M000317073

Steven Alvarez is originally from Safford, Arizona. He studied English and creative writing at the University of Arizona and at the Graduate Center, City University of New York. His poetry has appeared in Fence, Drunken Boat, Shampoo, and was recognized by the Poetry Society of America's Poems of Times Square. He teaches English at Queens College, City University of New York. He lives in New York City.

Foto de portada: © Kim Strong (Piece of the Museo Aecheologico Nazionale di Cagliari)
Diseño de colección: Albán Aira

© Todos los derechos, Editorial Paroxismo

Queda prohibida la reproducción parcial o total del contenido de esta edición sin el consentimiento del editor.

All rights reserved. No part of this publication may be reproduced without permission in writing from the publisher.

Impreso en Estados Unidos de América

ISBN 978-0615545912
Library of Congress Control Number: 2011939808

Primera edición de *The Pocho Codex* de Steven Alvarez publicada en 2011.

The Pocho Codex:
Piercing an Amurkan Poetic Historiography

Steven Alvarez

Editorial Paroxismo

C O N T E N T S

/ the blood of this body is that of the mineral veins of the
Amurkan kingdom

Quetzalcoatl went east.
Cortés came from the west.
Wetbacks go north.
The dead go south.
Those are the cardinal points of Mexico,
and no one can escape them!

Carlos Fuentes

CONQUISTADO

CONOCIMIENTO

REQEZA

FUERZA

.Tuesday.**m a r t e s / 4 Rain / 1211 hrs**

& SHE thinking watching Chaley sleep
      / of crawling inside

                Chaley like Jonah inside that
                big

    pinche Godfish /   SHE wonders how

      to walk barefoot wd feel /
                / stepping thru Chaley's
stomachlining
          right now
      / tequila puddles . . . sange de madre

          she smiles /
              yellow teeth
    crooked bottomrow nice little humph to her laugh

    & ahhh her teeth's ridgedridged
          spiked haircombs
                    espines collapsing building
          striations

          of ¿golden?   bad breath

          ay dios—
    [faint accordion whispers somewhere floating maybe like smoke
          sublte nortecuense smoke]

¿How does she fit yr existence / sleepy Chaley? sleeping sleepy Chaley ? / /

          pobresita postcoital nonpocha Xochitl Flores can't
sleep
          & plus for mostly seven hrs straight stared steadily
at ceiling
          & possibly at him whose güero gabacho organs
          touched hers already thrice
& then **than than tharán** CHALEY CHASTITELLEZ (as they still sing of him[1]) slow

---

[1] In cantinas & countrystores. In those ranchos where viejitos gather at cool dusk w/ Johnny Walker red passed around clockwise smokin & listenin to old canciones & cuentos of other days. "He breaks before he bends—& cuts a dashin figure" dijeron these old bastards. "A man a man 'twas a man." They also make albures abt his "stuffing his own shaved scrotum in his mouth puro huevón ja ja JA." A huevo: "another Latino Dedalus—what this world needs eh" / "slightly Byronic in slouch / more Oneigen in shape" / "belonging to that most vile category of social fauna / human rubbish" / yes at times / "claims life hostile to him" / "& so harbors brown resentment" / "mapped betweeness folks in this business call it / & where Dedalus had god & Ireland / he's got Guadalupan Aztecs / & Massico" / "& both shape poetry" / "when born his pappy sd 'this pinche huevón will be a poet—look at the size of his mouth' / & right then still slippery w/ his birthjuices his pappy lifted that chavalito & dedicated him to the Sun & to that flowery death of poetry / so sure enough he's here sung abt / & sings too" / of his "sexploits" of course / but here save for yr heart those favorite ditties of old men in country stores a-shootin the shit where C's phallic obsession becomes symbolic of organic sexual masculine forceful power / phallocentri potency / come el Mickey Mouse / & those *corridos* of his exploits / his conquests / w/ accompanied gritos / as he grabs his crotch & making

opens & closes & opens & closes his
     sticky pulpy eyes o p e n & light
eyecrusts /
    slow exercises lashes & away   open/close/ open &
        g o n e   he   stretch—yaaawn

rotates head to his left slow
    as she stares at him   still   s i g h / ay / & O shit vision of smile arriving all at

once /
             Xochitl smiles
              Xochitl
                 s t i l l

       & he thinks [slow] this instant (shit) one ye
            think closest slow rather one   YAWNNN
            living furthes—YAAHWN slow O shit

      &: sacri-sacri-sacrifice seemingly essentially same shit
      &: this Nahua flor keeps me slow company O shit

          &: pues ¿what cd be better than company?—

      &: so warm / ¿verdad?
          sordo
              mamacita /

P U E S es complicao y Chaley es un poco cabrón   {   ‘

                  |

                       sota

                       linda—

& waking w/ dryhot tequilafumes in his mouth
    our güero barero Chastitellez
    reckons beauty is brown brown beauty Xochitl
        like old lyrics in one way   at this early instant

---

pelvic thrusts repeating "este / mama este" / yes / his "terminology abounds in sexual allusions which reveal his
phallic obsession / his sexual ogan becomes symbolic of his masculine force" / Ramos 1962: 59-60 / pues /
aggression / y la vida es una chinga

O Tuesday / noon O &
    as words worth retelling   as soundsense   pues immense
                    &: yes found his way into her pants—
"Good mornin Chaley
                              presses smallpalm to his baldchest

                         "Yo / mornin—
CUE : scene / in terms of reduplication y complicacíón(es) /
      plastic & neon   drank too many pinche hidalgos one
      obsidian / stones   after another last nite—& yesyes w/ eyes & yes
      / bones / &   w/ sufficient suavity & severe suerte
      skin   / drums   yes on his side & w/ her clearly

      & hornshells   drunken también sí
                                  SÍ :
                          c o m p a n y[2]

              carajo: he only wished his jokes ended in absurdity

(audience) E--------------se /
            CA------------------brón
                            ¡GO! /
          YEAH   GREEN-¡GO!

      &: that bad idea catches up w/ ye this day / this Tuesday rainday C
                 & how ye sd to yr drunken self Chastitellez last night
           shit   roam   forth
           down
                 whilst   stinging a in history weaving
           blankets from her hair   verdad un chinga blankets
      from her hair
           I cd weave tonight
                 that not yr worst fear
                 ye don't want—lo /
                     SOFT
                she speaks—
                 dejando de chingaderas[3]
"love you cariño"

---

[2] **MEX'D FOR NOTHING:**
to think / when one's no longer mocoso / when one's not yet viejo / that one's no longer young / that one yet is not yet viejo / that's perhaps something—to pause / sí símon /toward the close / to close / to pause / close of one's houred día / & consider darkeneing oriente / brightening sleep / SLEEP / the pleasure pleasure because it was / the pain paid it shall be / the glad acts grown orgulloso / yes / the sueños / the proud acts grown stubborn / the panting / the trembling towards being / gone / being / to come / yeah & founding / & the true true no longer / still / & the false true yet not / & to will not to smile after all / sitting in sombras / hearing cicadas / willing night / still / no swishing / no moving / hablando / yes / all this again / otra vez /no not again / no no it's not heart shit-for-brains / no it's not liver pendejo / not spleen either fatass / no its not thank god prostate cabrón / no it's not ovaries fuckface / no it's muscular a su puta madre / it's nerfous [sic]—then gnashing ends / or it goes on / & one's in the pit / in the hollow / shit / the longing for longing gone / gone / shit / the horror of horror / still / sleep / SLOW /& one's in the hollow / shit /at the foot of the hills at last / the ways down / up a tree's crotch / the ways up / down & free / at last / ándale sale /for an instant at last / still & last / sleep & nothing at last / &c—BUT w/ COMPANY no none of this O no no
[3] "The Mexican macho is a humorist who commits *chingaderas* / that is / unforeseen acts that produce confusion / horror / & destruction / he opens the world / in doing so / he rips & tears it / & this violence provokes a great sinister laugh"—ja JA—"the humor of the *macho* is an act of revenge [. . .] essential attribute of the *macho*-power almost always reveals itself as a capacity for wounding / humiliating / annihilating" PAZtlán 1961:81 / "if there is no joke in the social structure / no other joke can appear" Douglas 1968:366

& Chastitellez sez : "igualmente mi vida"

palabra)   (porque los hombres tienen la última

&   ¿what don't ye need in yr life?

That. This. Her.

Here. Las Vegas /
      Bally's   pues :   **faraway palaces of**
plastic & marble

                       drink
              gamble eat
                      S E X

eat drink gamble
                      S E X
       E S O

       -refrán-

eat drink
       G A M B L E   sex

E A T   drink   sex
              gamble
         eat   D R I N K
              sex   drinkÓ R A L E
                       gamble
              sex
E A T
                                drink
              gamble
S E X
                   eat   D R I N K
gamble
                   S E X X X
         eat
         drink   G A M B L E
         sex
                   E A T   drink
         gamble   S E X
eat   drink
         g   amble   S E X

& then
neonflash & blinkflicker clash
         keyclick heelclack doorcrack
         crash click lick lash lick mmmm

thig thag thob thuzzle

locked alone in hotelroom locked bodies
                    sweat

         & last nite on balcón
         red desert wind
         her blue dress
         blowing

         from her cankles [sic] God & Sr. Chastitellez

            stuck two fingers inside her

            haciendo disco dirty
            hanky-pank dancefloor
               cochinadas
            piglike ways
               his chorizo
            harder than the times of '29[4]

PERO Chaley yr brownblood
        flows gabacho
        slow & deep / & Xochitl / sun companion
        morena [mostly] hermosa[5]

&: near her now her brownbeauty last nite nearly forgotten
    so don't equate her skincolor now to yr Mextizo nation breeding
    & pues pinche gafas despues cervezas para thee wey

    yet Chaley directly fragmatically evokes
              returning drunk from
                  under that volcano

    w/ Xochitl last blackhawk / as / obsidian night
    & promising to hace cummings
           in her mouth (DONE & DONE

    no compassion de tí   **hijo ye got a mouth on ye**
    &: inside her

                           sí y la mugre no se
    & stayin   **acabó ¡ó!**
in her pouch long after he spit his soul
            limp
            hhhmppphh—ehhhah
                 ¡*BLAST*!—blessed romantic explosion
                 finished horchata satiation
                 sensation proud soldier
                 for our Lord Quetzalcoatl's Reconquista

---

[4] Grosería list for later . . .

[5] No hay mujer fea / solo bellas extrañas. Voice from afar: "Qué naco."

cabrón

"todo se ha fuckin jodido
"menos el gotdamned amor he sd
after minutes

1st postcoitally tryin to form sentences
in broken espanglish
blood drained from brain & as noted his soul

spit inside her—ándale
"Yrs truly / he sd / "papi chulo
she chuckled catching her own breath

—plus one messy saltstain he left on her tumtum—

aún ayer en lastnight :
yea birdsong Xochitl
& aloud :
"birdsong / yr
"face / leaf
"falling [touching her cheek
tenderly kissing
her lips yes closely together softly]
but **NO** she's his mariposa

& internally:
¡N O W!
R I G H T
AHORITA
¡NO!⁶

---

⁶ **SINNNN:**
No
No no
No
No
Noooo
Nono no
No
No No
No
Nooooo O nooo O ooophump no no no nonn nuh **n n n n n no**
N
No
O
No no no no nonononononononnooooo
No
No
Noooooo
Now her turn on teop he sez to hi—
Nooo
No
No
No
NO
Noooooooooooooooonietenu
all Chaley wanted: una jipiteca—
¿Que Honda wey?

[cincuentacinco : EN CHINGA / aye bato ándale]

"touching red air / dust

      "& soft as grass livid & bright as dayshine
        "hands on yr face mine
      "my fingers pulsing life & I see sky in yr cara
        "& tomorrow amor
          "Weds / & that's six lifetimes
          "away baby / "

    "no me jodas Chaley" she sd

          b/c Xochitl cd
        see thru his eyes / which as
          he whispered dulceless nothings

rested on her culo / glassy / somewhat sunny "I think y're lleno de mierda"

"MIRE XOCHITL" Chaley sd

when first they met sitting next
to one another at this
Texican casino[7] bar
down the road a piece
from the strip
/ los dos solos
"economics: more than supply
"&
"demand /but touching arms /
"ramas / symbolic baby
"roots baby / limbs baby
"/NOW
"THAT'S unison mujer

"& ye can't supply time /

        "¿verdad?"

a l l   t h e   v a t o   n e e d e d   t o   s a y
        [¿ ?]

"& ¿y're Mexicano?" she asked

    "mahs Amuricahno kay Mecksicahno / pedo poodo Mecksicahno mahs
    "o maynos mahs maynos kay mahs / in other words

---

[7]Beer-goggled Chaley: no entiende that this casino wd bring darkness to life

"puro Pocho[8] de Pochtlán / Mecks—er Mayheekhano
"perdón my humid Amurkan tongue's
"inability to rrrrrrrrroll . . . mis eres/

"my people[9] wandered from south
"Al Norte & stopped to set
"up shop when they saw some

"falcon rip into two turtles
"three rabbits / & this unlucky
"pug pup in cactustree shade
"this up near Bisbee AZtlán[10]
"maybe you've heard of it
"y mis abuelos sd in Spanish
" 'this is our land / AZtlán'
"but that copper mine there
"shut down dried up
"big hole in AZtlán's center now
"Lavender Spit dried up 1974
"& for hot copper
"mis padres marched on
"for seven legendary cities
"for but a few years
"& miles more north
"hours north
"& indeed they found their
"nopal shooting from stone
"& settled in 1980 & by
"2005 paid off their mortgage—
"livin that Amurkan Dream—yeah

"that's right they set out to conquer
"New AZtlán so promptly
"& directly my parents walked
"into WallMart INC/ AZTLÁN straight
"thru electric sliding doors & desert
"hotwind into climate controlled
"amiability this was around 1990—my timing's bad right now understand
"(estoy pocito pedo)
"but / like I sd I'm er greingo [sic] / pues
"gabacho"

---

[8] Burnin contempt for different ancestries & Amurkan hauteur to Makesicko & toward old country güeys / vatos needed to be superior to something eh / but then self segregation from both cultures & that's one lost race b— where's his pocha fresa anyway he asked to lock & make one brown body desmade / & wedged between a pyramid & skyscraper

[9] LONG LINE OF COWARDS FROM SINAL♡A / but de costra y cáscara de la casta Castilla

[10] AZtlán "place of whiteness" where wanderin began & returned chosen desert godforsaken land FOR:
¿don't ye know
that in Arizone
by law our most Sovereign Lord
of Heheheaven & all Earth right here by four poles
thus enclosed /
that w/in this unending AZTLÁN spicsphere AZtlán shines in majesty & splendor?

"ah sí"

    /touched his arm

[hecho en /
[estados unidos /
pendejo]

"y're so güero"[11]

y claro /

cabrón

a veces

    & C: thanky kindly w/ latin sangre de madre verdad

        b/c he cd turn off Pochisme when necessary

    & after all he smelled greengo enough wearing his
    Old Spic aftershave & hear that Tejano Top 40 . . .

& b/c alcohol clearly affects speech rate & instensity / phonological precision /
    general body disposition memory & inhibition
& thusly Prince Chaley [vocalizing something or other—mayhap

[routhe which ofte konne taketh heede]

w/ money from his Messican roots
purchased this creamy sunlit damsel 4 d. julios / 4 tzihuacs / un pulque
    del chamaqueron /
    3 xx micheladas /
  & 2 car bombs irlandés
    & Chaley blushed

    & Xochitl laughed
    & Chaley cursed bloody carajo al gobierno
    & Xochitl laughed
    & Chaley stood
    & Xochitl gazed up
& she seyd to this white caballero who came from el sol w/ (drunken)
sun of her own in her obsidian eyes
    "take me in yr arms & ROCKET ME—

¡ BENEDICITE !

& more : "—we're a-makin starlove tonite mi vida—"

---

[11] his upbringing
    fostered qualities expected to generate
    symbolic benefits—rewards—of someone
    w/ light skin / the affluence
    of standard English / & the subtle
    dissentegration
    of any chains
    brown

¡ ÁNDELE !

¡ ALAS !

PUES—QUE

¡SÍ!¹²

pero befoure this
   our heroe had to aske

               te quiero un chingo

himselfe
    one important question

     certes her name he forgot

           certes her familie
           unknowne & Chaley uncertyn

     alas his
     focalized object twisted

        somtyme convoluted
        /focalized
        gaze tortuous fro drinkie &
           cigarettes smoked
        too many (filterless)

        bueno: perspective alle wrong

    sith : "have pitie on me . . . I fogot yr name
    & starlove Xochitl Flores: "no importa

    hearts
        heard
hard
        lusts
             there debajo

    the pinche volcán

hang it all mister *enfant terrible*

   & so off they wandered to her Bally's room

---

¹² "harder than hardest marble to moans" Garcilaso de la Verga's *Égloga I* / 1.57

to make el beast w/ 2 backs   **sí es la verdad**

& decorated on her Bally's pad's walls
arrows fletched w/ quetzal plumes / heron
plumes / troupial plumes / roseate
spoonbill plumes / flamingo
plumes / cotinga plumes   **no manches**
güey
& tortoise shells of varying
shades & sizes

qué extraño
but less strange
images of James Dean / el Elvis / & Vincente Hernandez
on two touching walls

& Xochitl threw him down & came
kissy kiss kiss
facedown upon   him
devouring him &   ripping
open his pecho
qué pachanga
scratching to hell his legs & arms[13]

& screaming ¡ Santiago !
¡ Santiago ! & dispatching
him thoroughly
even despite his fair swordplay

CHALEY CHASTITELLEZ

YOU DID IT

(& so easy too!)

---

[13] **EL PRIMO dijo**

P R I M O

T L A C U I L O
el es como las iglesias:
todas son llamadas amisa
y pocas son elegidas /

no es mentira: todas son elegidas pa' el

& despues

for Chaley as he slept w/ right delight
deep ajocandando :

in first place   her skin
too hostile   *turned treebark   she ran*
to be   *to stay from skinbreak*
lyrical   *of that goddamned god-man*
          looking to stuff his lownose

into her pure hole   SHE turned
into oak
brickfaced
tears   tho he poked her
in her new arbolhole
into her knot
actually her backscum
& she swelled /

& tears trickled from her leaves

—together & eternal yea
& relocated w/ his mistress
—housed in highest heavens
level thirteen condo w/ balcony overlookin
beautiful neonsmoke chaos
& in their big bad bed

they begot Tezcatlipoca MORENO
Tezcatlipoca RED Quetzalcoatl GÜERO
y Huitzilopochtli BLUE (known here
as Blue Star[14] /

¡ A W A K E !   ¡ O !
¡ Lo ! real . . . maravilloso
dicesquetevas / /
eyecrusts eyecrusts flutterflutter
sigh
& he abruptly wakes he then gladly for / because
beautiful /

pleasant vision & because
promised [¿ ?] victory / & on
his
battle-standard / battle
formation [¿ ?] dios
to honor
WHOA he sez / ¿God still here help me Guadalupe? to himself
he turns to his side / toward her / her

---

[14] whom C searches
for in Vegas getting drunker &
drunker before meeting Xochitl

cinnamonred neck / her heaving reddish neck
her brownish visage & he notices acne on her chin
still here—shit—al at once her face her stare /
O shit slowly slow slow C sez to self

& in his brainglobs : slow ye don't need these things sez C steady
to self   s l o w   now entirely awake   YES   Yawwwnnnuh
things right now mean trouble
O   s l o w

thinks of running some far place fast   ahorita en chinga
maybe Manhatitlán
to see himself quickly dodging weeds & women
como this morena volcán Xochitl

so cold   turns back 'pon his back his gnarled knees knock

under blanky

feet freeze   & as he
marvels her yellow dagger choppers / he

thinks this Xochitl's got that convulsive beauty

—but alas we cannot be—
Forsooth I need to get
the fuck out of here he   **Y're slime sir**
nods his head

"¿did ye dream?" she asks him

/ wd rather suffocate already than breathe her water /
& anyway maybe cd be rain of fire tonite
always always that threat / yet
more likely evaporating neonrain & hot neonmoon—
"d-dreamt when I met you—everyone smimming in
"ocean/ but I clung to some ropebridge"

& she: "¿yeah?"
qué divine
& C: "yea girl sound of my bloodocean / but I clung to
"catch my heavy heaved breath
"down there in my greenlean guts
"& to breathe water ye
"slid into my sorespace—
"everyone swam in w/ yr dark/ curious fringe   ¿?
"sucked the breath right out of me ye
"know me in yr eyes
"my fear"

some sorta

sigh she emits [¿ ?]

pure poetik rhetorik on his part
(& now to drop akademik :

WHEN we observe

any discourse
or discursive exchange
we ASK

these materialist questions

at RHETORIK's roots

¿W H O deploys W H I C H discourse thru
W H A T means

in W H A T time & place
addressing W H I C H **situation**
& W H I C H **human subjects**
for W H A T **purposes** & w/
W H A T **outcomes?**

[perswasion

W H O : el baboso Sr. Chastitellez

W H I C H : sloppy highmod/Chicanory poetix [since
[Realism's but a comfortable disease

W H A T : por la boca símon que sí* & print pues

W H I C H : postcoital chitchat shit

W H I C H : más o menos fictional hermosa Nahua

flower

W H A T : in case to make beast otra vez

W H A T : **yup**)

/END RESULT/

cu-cu-umminnnnn uh inside her a-a-again—again—
cochinos
& leavin soon after coming immediately on his mind
but before this &
laying side to side his arm around her his mind
a-swirl Xochitl confesses /
sinvirgüenzas

her hosbond serves
this Amurkan military en Irak

er . . . ¿mierda?[15]

POS POS POS   how she offers what folklorists call
                that greater Mexican materialist rhetorik
                    of one good & reliable neighbor
importuned & sighed for / Chaley looks at her closely at her teeth
                & imagines swaying
                    in nocturnal wind   no reason why

for just—little well . . .
                despite everything / deadman alas

                & Xochitl understonds his eyen two
                so she mentions not her daughter

                & she sees him shot w/ ghosts
                    not unhappy mind
                    but somewhere else

                & tho she's known
                    him but nine hours
                    she understonds his
                brainsways / waves
                    & how & how

                he must be poetik w/ that
                    prosody he effects   **Chaley wonders if Xochitl**
                    or her listenin pleasance   **spends more time**
                                                    reading poesy
well fine 3rd sun mess this all   **or masturbating**
                Chaley tells Xochitl—"¿mind if I take away
                                                        then Chaley
                "some them jadebones / mi vida?
                                                    wonders if

                                                    Chaley
                & Xochitl sez "pues—1st blow on my concha 4X /   **spends more**
                    "& if ye make me smile / ye can have anything
                                                    time reading

                        "me included   **poesy**

                                                    or
& SO : Chaley stayed down there for 20-25 / twice she shuddered
                                                    aprietiendo
        & afterward she bathed him & sat him
                                                    el cuello al
                on her bathmat of flamingo plumes

---

[15] Aye ¿bebe cay passOH? thought I's yr only vato / ni modo

ganso

      & wrapped his wethead w/ red bands

& he appreciated soon enough that Xochitl's husband
  wd smash his face w/ a rabbit jar

                & after "I'll have a glass of Tzihuac / por favor

    as he sits on sofa feet propped up
    misc papers there on coffetable
    "I like these reed coasters
    Chaley sez yes
  have courage Xochitl

    he thinks / ah
    w/ lips of men
she scatters her flowers—w/ tears of melancholy flowers

we'll get thru this sure enough[16] & as he watches her pour
  his Tzihuac in her brown bathrobe he thinks
        yes Xochitl "Chastitellez" wd make one good & industrious mate
        / or he thinks she's fit to be ruled
          & that undeniably she *is* textually attractive if he
          cocks his head & dims his eyes askance those
          texty hips
          texty lips
          & stretchmarks on sides of her huge
          floppy texty chicharrrrones
          her two-dimensional
          geometrikally absolutely textually stimulating
          nalgas / & suddenly España[17]—musa España—his name for his
menso
      member
      quakes . . .
  & since he thinks he might squeeze one more in . . .
      / ah there's the rub /
  —blue thunder running thru his system or something[18]—
he stands & walks to his pants / boner guiding his way
          removes moleskine from backpocket
          & writes in his notes:
          LINE: *crazy ones don't sleep*
          at night La Pelona that gringa
          amiga never slept at night & who he
          never saw in any July

          let down her sweaty hair & **CONQUER**[19]

---

[16] As if in an exagmination of conscience

[17] España: what goes up must come down . . . gradually

[18] Chaley / keep yr pecker up / whatever the detail

[19] GOD creator in highest heaven permits this conquest / in order that she may know him & come out from her
infamy / this bestial & diabolik life she leads / 'tis for this *rAZtlánón* that Chaley subjugates her vast host /
                  eh / en CHINGA we trust
                      we must thrust
                      be dust
            & lust be blessed
                      as best bodybeast questions answered

what ye don't want
poet / VOMIT / shit / let her
      drink water
        from yr mouth

ye need not take back her past

kissy musty

she's already been colonized

tangling tingling tongues

(apologize pull out her eyes

pues pues pues
& he puts his notebook away & enough thinks ni modo
    then briefly toughly tells himself echate el palo de

una vez más **cabrón**

    & then that Xochitl's *husband* is the real cabrón
    & O devasted world / as he returns to sofa
    & as he sits he recalls that birdsnake vision before
    he met Xochitl but shakes his head /
& asks himself ¿who's this woman?
& Xochitl asks what abt those coasters as she eases her way
    next to poet & hey look at those womanly hips
HEY she sez & Chaley marvels that yes she's good w/ width
    & YES she opens his boxerhole

HALLO ESPAÑA

  & she whips him out
but directly he reaches for—yes—silver ashtray
& places España onto it
  & serves himself to her
for Chaley / puro caballero / is always willing to donate his

organ /

smiles at his Johmpson [sic]:
"hallo my li'l sympol scepter of poder
  "& fecundity—

"lookin erect & prestigious ¡SUN!—"
Xochitl laughs at this
& Chaley sez "sometime too hot the eye of my pipi shines . . ."
Xochitl laughs at this "¿de veras?"
  "¿do ye read poetry or masturbate more?"
Xochitl laughs at this "¿de veras?"
  "¿why you laughing? That's a serious question mujer"
Xochitl laughs at this "¿de veras?"
  "yes yes day verdhas yes" he sez "pues
  "day vedhas y can calavedhas pues pos pues"

pues

& his quests for conquests yes
Nota: El Secreto para conquistar a una mujer es conocer algo en ella que los demás ignoren

2.2

                                           (tu poin tu)

a

          ¡Oyé! ¡Oyé! ¡Oyé! ¡Oyé!

                     she
             w/ subtle smile
                   hauteur / & secret savage

     +

          +

          Chaley

                 +
              coming

         double
          flower lure
         foul +
           +   flower song slower slung all
wrong

                                            thinks in

English he reckons[20]

---

[20] in this as well & they finish before he leaves for his flight to AZtlán his home to forget this all

b

Joyous revelry opinion of Lefebvre / ¡súsia!   B A S T A

/ look: here too we find

a/symmetry[21] :
self[22] seeks[23] other[24] each *person*[25]
finding[26] other[27] while . . . d—[28]
what *person*[29] seeks[30] in
self[31] /
   nostalgia[32]
repeats[33]
pure love[34] always[35] disappoints[36] / inconceivable[37]
apart[38]
      tendency[39]
         & release[40] of original[41]

—

[21] fe/male
[22] & latent
[23] glory glory plural belles
[24] from flesh reversing original
[25] seeks self in hopes of
[26] vestiges of
[27] tension / replaces tensions w/
[28] like red nochebuenas
[29] ¡ATENCIÓN! ¡ATENCIÓN! ¡ATENCIÓN!
[30] illimute
[31] other is project of
[32] absolute love
[33] to relative love
[34] O god / head he thinks & in a metasort of way
[35] END W/ DESTRUCTION BY RAIN OF FIRE / FIRE STICKS / TRANSFORMED INTO BIRDS 312 years ¡
ATENCIÓN !
[36] When systemic organization gets a-cluttered / too noisy / & all sd filled w/ failure / aggression / devising denials /
lying in dark w/ eyes closed tight / body writhing
[37] burden to follow no doubt—severe betrayals /   ¿but to whom?
[38] **4 water** 676 years transformed into fish
[39] life total / limit
[40] [ahgasm]
[41] O holy Gadjam / that's one theory of everything / beautiful universe / *dissolve*

c

I AM first man of Quetzalcoatl

I am Quetz-co himself

        mija   sez C to X   C: 22 yrs

                                            X: 23 yrs

                        . . . manifestation as well as man   *digo: I*

accept myself entire

size of AKlaska entire

                        & proceed to make my destiny
                                ¿why?

                        ¿what else can I do?

d

Chaley writes
/ / / // /

"see to it ye be not one ratgnawed gourd"

& more

know

disposed so as to know that I know & don't want to

that you know & don't want to know that I know
& do not want to know that you will give me my

desired countergift

yes she blooms
 come get this you
como quieres tu

d.2

flipped script
condensed & refined / good
friend listen . . . avoid
yr guard for thunder sd in her lively vivid   voice show me show me
show me

total war growing slowly in her mind's heist

& so he crept effortlessly[42] & she around limped[43] night drifted drifted
from twone

& they drank & got drunker he the mountain she the river

& cyclic series of trials by night funny customers cutting rugs

tippin mugs of pilsner & ale couple kinder playing nightgames drawing circles of
mama's

cervix later murdering their parents even customers hardly ask loosely—¡POOF!

never mind abt the pee all over the floor from little girls probably no more than
fourteen

he caught equally matriculating—how wd one run for public office

w. such a record?

¿what the?

---

[42] slept down
[43] pulsing dripping

nothing to be peripatetic poetic emergence

& this machine run amok

economy driven warfare & cultural production

reproduced recirculated received reinterpreted

& in all rearticulated / respoken / rewritten

dicen que reinscribed / but now think abt kinetic

darkness /

disc

farce   larceny

sic.   Legacy

wordswords

see he sworded words into bi-syllababels fellowed hand dropped

into ¡O our patrocotic they!

e [écrit au crayon]

609—narrative

605 = = = sun shone whole sure

613 = = = = = = = = = dont shut me up in prose prophecy (n. gaddamnit)

216   86

571—different /

restraint—form—sound—

318

321   then   591—magnetic sea / stimulate earth

318   322

320

312

492—leopard—Locke—movement—wind—ecology

576 / / /

———

585

remember to hinder ye

& ye to bind me

& drop me bone by bone

605

Amurka / / / Yorope / / / AMURKA AMURKA

AMURKA

f [657]

                                     no

                             mountains

no oceans no birds   no train   salmon

sky   no   no   no   sun   no purple

no colors no smells no window

nobody—certainly no

    AZtlán

V

g

ong [sic]

ago Chastitellez invaded fertilized

crescented desert

<u>wasteland</u> & soaked

splendid identity

gentle warm spoils

Qoooophew &

Chaley

Chastitellez rode

coasters over constituted Tigrisland

shook hands

had his photo taken

w/ grownfolks & mayors

who worked

long hours (a)

costumed in

traditional cuneiform (b)

garbed

history of

might-ve been   for

skyline her father

had no

equal   yikes

g.2

at bodega-rico

from school

of beauty lookin

out window at

moonshine face

g.3

book of

ideas

red Tezcatlipoca

mist

world

fire

heroes

hymn

black Textcatlipoca

life

Quetzalcoatl

glory

genius   passion

(1)

(2)

Huitzilopocho   blood

h

shinin shhh

eeeee lookin

in she lookin

out

Xochitl instantly

wondered

abt her dream

to Chaley sleepy Chaley

this morning

upon his sleeping

& she stood

in his palm

he looking down

on her

she cd

easily fit

      inside his nostril

    she cd

practically see

his entire brain

as she gazed

up his

nostril & she

sd to him

in her small pipe

I'm here

to bring

ye images

for yr verses

[margin: "& vices"]

Chaley b/c

I love

ye so now

much as snow

so tell me

you love

me & kiss me

here & here long

& hard   GO

his desiccated

torn

puckered lips

descended

to devour her

w/ love

she woke

h.2

SING cantante sing of agency
inventively scripted & deployed
bounding over walls
SING phallosophically
of mythico dick wagging
& of overdetermined golden papilla
SING of sexuality / yes & this one's
enormity of His-pano heteronormity
SING puro macho /
quién quiere to gravitate
neurotic toward erotic
performing roles in sexy
dramas con mestiza chavalas y
gringa damas & embracing
patterns in his limited repertoire
SING SING misgilded essential dimensions
yea / SING of typecast Latinos   **en estereo pues**
& SING of his mythos powerful
underling underlying intimate
need to surrender solace
for desire & to ravage
women O cruelly / c o l o n i a l l y[44]
ol school hegemonically
                    / yet he thinks himself discontent w/ politiks
y e p a   pues . . . yes—well
                                            / / / /
            S I N G of Chaley Chastitellez /   **sing**
            how this hoss   **¡GODDAMN!**
  constructs & deploys
from deep in his pocho
crotch his object seeker—
puro vaquero chorizón
sinvergüenza
—sneakier than una culebra
& how in his pocket
part of this Other (or entonces part
of *an*Other)
extends eroticized
& his lifelong quest
yes for connectedness
  /
aún some mess
  /

& his oneness

---

[44] **ONE THEORY OF THE POCHO CODEX:**
es importante que me escuches: what ye always ever knew now nasty neophytes / neither neanderthall nor fail better
Epik fabricator / another spikin' glyph prophet pledge / another pariah prayer prose curve / in some sensical tradition
/ of constraint combatactiks Xicanery despondent baroque hallucinations & naked branches / LOOK: this dance of
conquest light has come to yr bedroom / so disrober yrself / & enters yes alas Capitan Chorizo . . . whispering sweet
nuthins in that vast common language(s) unitin all Amurkans.

The Pocho Codex

/

    g   o   n   e

i

my god

what Chaley

asked slipping on

his sock

  & she w/ his scrotum interdigitalis

saw something headless

w/ absolutely nothing to do

& in one another's arms

they their ignorances beheld as cloudly ceiba trees above wrapped round them gripping them closer hard he still had hardly sd he sd anything he knew she clearly knew all to say & he'd always just agreed never attempting to expound childhood's childlike charm Chastitellez whose ancestors walky-walked from somewhere North Norte they sey AKlaska they sey then south to Makesicko then back northward again pues Al Norte whence those borders solidified . . . but los antepasados who walky-walked down w/ chicanery down great desert Snornora [sic] down down down to Mexica w/ but two gallons of water & three redbulls

[margin: Chaley: *laments / sorrows eats out his heart when he acknowledges how he offended them . . . how he's wronged em / takes fright / terrified*]

guided by that Koyote Huitzlipocho who passed them all thru then there in Naco / & in doing this first dressed them in ostrich boots / & belts w/ buckles of escorpións / & polyester cowboy pants / & two gold rings on one hand at least / teaching them to pepper every phrase w/ either cabrón or some form of ching

& naturally all yawned but strongly & finally they dug roots on water & built their city 'pon lake: homeland yea: that old quest for homeland & struggle in fields of wicked wildernesses along that way & carving up a bit of political power starving & thirstin among dangerous animals & thorny wildernesses disputed & divided / called by Huitzlipocho on these Xicanos followed until Snake Mountain / disputed angles / how horizontals & verticals coincided / until they saw some great eagle perched upon cactus / & in its beak bore nopalfruit / stylized humanheart / painted in books they created & carried / bones & precious feathers of many bright birds / brilliant as those of Tollan / painted pages / hearts living in painted pages

                              still throbbing singing royal fibers in textiled deerskins w/ princes who wd dance & thereby command the discourse of all contexts and histories of all water / those ancestors they point in those codices created ye / uttered ye like some flowers into existence / commas spewing from their lips / painted like song / those artists as ancestors / whose books came burning to ends now nearly complete & yes those ancestors: bones mostly now ashchunk coals dwindling now past hottest whitetime now simply windscraps for that heathen who begot SEE BELOW & shortly [margin: "then / güey güey back then ahem"] *whence priests arrived cloaked in their deer's skins & blackfaces of ashrub of*

Camaxtli-Mixcoatl (tall brownbootsteppydout) up as their footprints

[MS *Codex Mojaodicus*[45]] *indica'o over shell necklace hill beyond to Coxcatlseven*

> > [MS letter holdings of Pancho Chastitellez estate / 13 Oct 1989]

in Tehuacan Valley games & deer & conejo hunts

> > > [MS interview transcription Pancho Chastitellez estate 9 Feb 1959]

& humansacrfices in name of Camaxtli-Mixcoatl [MS *Codex Mojaodicus*]

enduring Quecholli kids held hands

[ate ballsports hipbouncing their (trans; ¿played?)]

places reserved where one cd stand for where &

¿how to get seven itty tittle of recokonin?

reckon this neighbors: as primogeniture their preferred system of passing parsed

generations lords gained legitimacy from direct descent reckons of ancestors born of

trees / caves / rivers / sky / classic citadels some killed on accounts of their

unreckonings at pubs quayside / stabbed in their eyes yes yes

on other handies eleciones por la gente indigenas followed best OUR avatar of

Camaxtli-Mixcoatl who emerged from dark sevencaves of Chcomoztoc w/ bearded

what looked like disheveled demokratikas

> > [Pancho Chastitellez estate / 13 Oct 1989]

self-recognition & me-memory fundamentals to identitas distinct from neighboritas

nameself[46]

to exist [MS *Codex Mojaodicus*]

mememoree self-recogito pas tiempo

---

[45] Ed: rhythm of groups / elements / sequences of tides / beats / seasons / of breaths / & beating hearts / da-DUM / da-dum / da-dum / da-DUM & so on /
[46] Ed. sounds (¡sounds! ¡swounds! ¡word heist of soundest sense!) lifted from *Wake*

pasteesh[47] core to rearrive vichy &

TABLE 1 STRUCTURE OF THE POCHO CODEX MANUSCRIPT folios material contents border [I] parchment opening complex [Iv] parchment blank complex 5 parchment drawing 1 complex 5V-6 parchment G1 simple 6' parchment drawing 2 complex 7-102 paper G2-100 simple 102v-[103'] paper blank simple [104-110] paper blank none [111] paper (lighter weight) blank none [1] parchment contents A-C complex 2 parchment contents D-E complex 3 parchment contents F-K complex 4 [missing] ¿parchment? ¿contents L-Z? ¿complex? of lighter weight and partially deteriorated

this might suggest that it was originally a flyleaf & was affected by absence of binding until all four folios of this table were placed at the end of the manuscript therefore original structure might have been: seven parchment folios 104 paper folios (7-[110]) & one flyleaf the absence of watermarks & fact that solid modern Amurkan binding was imposed in 1987 prevent heartless detailed study of manuscript's structure particularly w/ regard to number format & distribution of gatherings however the coherence of the musical contents of ff. 7-102 confirm that no significant alteration was made after the manuscript was copied border drawn on most pagesas can be seen in the degree of elaboration of the border is related to the purpose of the page those containing music have a simple border consisting of five parallel lines & small circular ornaments all the parchment pages except those con-taining music have more elaborate borders of variable com-plexity, with floral and geometrical motives borders have also been drawn on pages w/ no content of these most striking is that verso of the opening folio ([IV]) which has a complex border though not as elaborate as other examples three pages at the end of the music also have simple borders & no other content these empty pages cd indicate that manuscript was never completed

[1595 / 12 wind]

March

A: GEOGRAPHY: legit copy / MS 47152h-1 Paper ink draft / Londres /

Yorope is a great place of verdure / of freshy fishy green / of wind / of
windy places / windy—a cold place . . . it becomes cold . . . much frost / a
place which freezes—a place from which such misery comes / where it
exists / a place of afflictions / a place of lamentations / of afflictions / of
weeping—a place of sadness / of compassionate sighing / which of course
spreads misery . . . of gorges in places / of crags—of craggy places / a place
of stony soils & souls / of hard soils & souls / but of soft soils & souls / a
most moist & fertile place / a place of peaks / of stone jungles / of dry
treestumps / a place of valleys / & a place as well of hollows—

a disturbing place . . . fearful
& frightful—of love / a dwelling place of serpents & rabbits & deer / a
place from which nothing departs / nothing leaves & nothing emerges / a
naturalist jacket of nothing place / not a place of ocelot / the cuitlachtli / the
bobcat / or the spider of prickly shrubs / nor of mizquitli / but yes of pine / a
place where the earth is owned by faceless beings / where the poor are
felled / of moats & kings & playwrights & torture

a place of crashing wind / of
whistling wind / whirlwinds of ice / gliding winds / a place where misery
abounds / a valley of hollows / a place where misery abounds / emerges /
spreads / is edible— [manuscript ends]

B: GEOGRAPHY: legit copy / MS 47152h-2 Painted deerskin / Jackson
Heights Queens / Assumed August [highly contested as exact continuation
of previous passage]

. . . forget Amurka [¡ !] & looky here at this sad Messico:

Messicko is a place of hunger—for in these Amurkas where hunger is born /
a home for hunger / death comes from hunger / place of trembling / of teeth
chatter / of green glass bottles clinking together & broken shards used as
wire fencing / a place of cramps & stiffening bodies / of fright / & flight /
constant fright / where one's devoured / slain by stealth / & abused—brutally
put to death / kidnapped / a place where one is put to death in the jaws of
the wild beasts of the land of the dead / a place of torment & where misery
abounds / & a calm place—of continuing calm—

skies: miserly / rains there rot soils / & lions small & cowardly /
there horses pigs & dogs become dwarves / where Yndios cold as serpents
have no souls / hairless despicable men / flabby degenerate beasts / make
children w/ their mothers

[manuscript ends]

[1992 / 5th sun / our present]

 honkey-tonk gringo corrido Gila Bend Corridor Bar / Gila Bend / AZTLÁN

                    s   t   r   u   m   [sic]

"for Chaley Chastitellez
    "that brave ballsy fellow
    "told those Xicanos
"working for la migra
"los vendidos agringados:
"'in Makesicko love
    "'germinates w/ the mouth
"'begins w/ the mouth
"'& her mouth the size of Puebla
"'w/ lips shaped like horizontal Sinaloas
"'& how beautiful her hips / two Chihuahuas—'
                            "¡ Z á s !
"& he proceeded to snap each of their necks
"one by one w/ swift judochops
                        "¡ Z á s ! ¡ Z á s ! ¡ Z á s ! ¡ Z á s ! ¡ Z á s !

"qué hombre"

            brasstipped snakeskin boots tap
                & a pouncing taxidermed bobacat lunges
            away from woodpanelled wall

"man's man / & for his Tío / a hero
"& for his Xochitl and La Muerte the salvador himself . . ."

                accordion accordion accordion

[2007 / 5th sun / our present]

OF HUMAN SACRFICE & SACRIFICAL DESCENT INTO HELL: legit
copy / MS 47158h-2 Paper ink draft / November

here in Mexico we find Chaley Chastitellez in McTlán after escaping
the treachery of creamy sunltit Xochitl Flores / who sd
to our knight "gud bai" after
his quote/unquote Great Refusal
& after many months after that rainy Tuesday
our fair Xochitl threw him down
& came kissy kiss kiss
facedown upon him
/ postVegas / many months
later tracking him to AKlaska
& murdering him—
devouring him & ripping
open his pecho   / qué pachanga /
scratching to hell his legs & arms
& screaming ¡ Santiago !
¡ Santiago ! & dispatching
him thoroughly
even despite (otra vez) his fair swordplay
then blackening his slowing
heart w/ copalsmoke
wrapped in nopales . . .

& now first stop / here / in Death's abode Chaley
finds himself presented w/ one of La Muerte's
jovencita emissary agents (of the four in anTlazoteteo
Cuaton / Caxxoch / Tlahui / or *Xapel* he can't determine)
& look: looking good for this pink pearl
of perfection appears painful /
                    her hair striped agate
                    clotted w/ blood into braids
                    never combed or parted
                    & her chocolatl eyes of pure stars
                    make no mistake freeze to the bone
                    & have the sun's seeing
                    & they sing rain / rain
                    & she swells him w/ embalmed songs
                    & up above: sagging moon / thick & pregnant

                    then she sez "no temas donde vayas
"que has de morir
"donde debes . . .
          "powerfully sacred / & when it FILLS OUR WORLD /
                    "yea
                    "like rayos of luz thru & thru"
& "hasta que tomé la píldora se me quitó el dolor"

          but her florid speech spoken to no one in particular—mind

Chaley hadn't sufficient Spanish to do w/ her & anyway
/ no / & ¡egad! ¡that smell!
& behold—¡Chaley Chastitellez!—
truchas yr name ¡ stinks ¡ sudden overwhelming stench
more than
carrion in Tuxson in July—
more than dead salmon filling dry creekbeds
in AKlaska in August—& he sickens & groans / folds
& darkness twists in him
like a river—weighing him down . . .
    & he contemplates again to go—yeah again—to leave
his hated & O so heated AZtlán . . .
—which he later does—claro—
but he continues on pulling himself along
dragging along some whitemud & on
passing this jovencita
voicing one gutteral grassy ass & smiling & suddently he strolls [sic ¿ ?]
further into his despondent baroque hallucination McTlanuense
until he reaches
that forested juncture [¿?]
& these cosmic trees—
fat & furbarked / w/ sky branches—
& he sits beneath one's shadows
which shines specks of stars & finds
a smoking mirror—he looks at his face
& this mirror cracks / & his face wrinkles
& he sees himself as puro viejo / face like a battered stone
& so he instantly sleeps—
later wakes—¿in his dream?
& he walks . . .   [margin: "& he wakes &c"]
        gritos de dolores sounding
        in his ears . . . death to gachupines &c [margin: "&c &c"]
& so he squats on a slab of unrefined copper to rest . . .
his hands leaning on this ore lump
& yonder AZtlán shining in the distance
he looking down from some height in space
of time / & as for space of space he's there where
his gaze lands
which as he sees & considers
effects tears to rush
into his eyes—
cold sobs cut his throat—
er / O . . . constructed tears
of smeared centuries gone
dripping down his
face & sorrowfully falling to stone
& piercing his heart—
        & as he wipes his face shadows
linger where his hands rest
 /
       & he wakes / ¿into another dream?
& who else but one-armed Álvaro Obregón

appears to him

& he looks up: banners reading "imposition / resistance / adaptation /
    "transformation"
"sound concepts güey" Obry sez then "¿where you goin?"
& immediately Chaley responds "to a place
 "of red daylight—to find some wisdom"
". . ." sez Obregón his mouth full of frozen blood
& Chaley wakes again—[¿ ?]
& again Obregón tho this time missing the opposite arm
"¿red daylight?"
"¿know it?"
"don't know" sez Obry—"but have a plug of this pulqazo—just fer ye"
"well I won't sey no" & he sips the brew from a yellow popote
sweet wine & sweeter still yet
& instantly / bien pedo / perfectamente drunk he falls
/ faints / on calle & dreams—sleeps—his snores
echo for miles in these canyons
& he ¿wakes? ¿dreams of waking?
& finds only silence—pure
& an empty rusted town of concrete
& rebar . . .
            & a new peak—btwn Popocatépetl & Iztaccíhuatl
& snow slowly descends
his face whitemudcaked . . .
& surrounded by carcasses
of books—pages lost among the dead
& that weight oppresses him—so he weeps
for these books—then
sings & his tears again endlessly cold
& long sighs issue deep from his guts
until he sleeps—
& he wakes—¿or dreams?—
to a beach—& there a hulk of serpents
formed into a raft—
& directly he reaches into his pocket
& produces his MTA Metrocard
which he promptly presents to the largest snake's
mouth / which it sucks & it slides
an entry for Chaley & he boards
& he sails into that diamond ocean
this boat gliding on burning waters
into that land of red daylight—
on the rim of the great sea
& his face reflects in ocean

[1519]

October-November / first handwritten pencil draft "[a] page so crowded that it is difficult for almost any reader, including its author, to unravel & decipher." Found encased in a wall at the Presidio in downtown Tuxson / where deyall got dem Arr-o-WAK cowboy hats / 1849 dated via carbon analysis / University of AZtlán 1979 / special collections library

POCHO MYSTIC TRIGRAMMES fer yr new world / old world / nowness

a

Skyday . . . young
   1st element grandfather / life / water
       sea-lakes / firesunheat—thunder
   mother of lightening & lightning
      wind wood   water
   cool moon
      mountain hinders movement
earth AZtlán cinnamon stars
   & elemental garb of grandmotherly destruction

¿espeak ye that langwedge of yr ancestors?

                 no güey not really

b   [1 Reed]

     los yropeos malos llegaron a Messico /

concrete dogs of
una Yndia she
suckled—each
time . . . black block
chihuahua at her feet
blue napkin attached
to her
ear "Xolo"
dramatic irony in
dimensions of
scale—¿verdad?
—umbilicus
connecting her to:
1) an embryonic host
2) an ear organ
3) a sink
4) a pelvis

c   [1520]

holding wolf's
neck / BURNING
 Aztec feet / eyes
upturned tears
         lopped brown hands gripped
in desperate supplication
reflected in tarnished
Yoropean armor
amputated & accumulated
in pits of other misc
bodyparts

[nota: each letter represents a
power of light & life]

[2008 / 5th sun / our present]

two translations of love poems transcribed from a partially destroyed codex
portion (*Codice Mojaodicus*) removed from the hot hilly poor & dry
Mexteca & now owned by some bald Bangladeshi guy named
Sarowar who lives in a studio apartment in Corona Queens just up the street
from the local rent-a-Mex / May-June

a

1 LINEAGE: legit copy, MS 47471a-2 Amatl paper screenfold fragment
painted both sides [second draft] / Early-mid November 1531 [¿ ?]

. . . . palimpestic . . . . .thy face . . . .
. . . .
. . . .
. . . . .
. . . . . . white dogs of dawn . . .
. . . .
. . . . .   & . . . . ¡ . . . . . .!
. . . . . command . . . .
. . . .
. . . . . . social inadequacy. . . . .
. . . . *per partes occidentales / ut dicitur / versus*
Yndia / in mari oceano

1) . . . .
2) . . . .

[3]) . . . .
. . . .
first urge . . . . stained sounds
. . . .
. . . . watch h . . rub . . . .
. . . . watch h . . rub / ¿los sonidos?
in h . . mouth . . . .
. . . . yn . . . . axictini
quinmahuiztilia iteohuan—
ica on huel huelitini
oquinxico in iyaohuan

. . . .
. . . .

. . . .
. . . . watch h . . rub ¿los sonidos? in h . . mouth . . . .
repeat . . . .
. . . .
. . . .
. . . .
eeeeatch / & wátchale watch / watch h . . rub ¿LOS
SONIDOS? in h . . mouth /

over & over / rubbing them into substance
/ . . . . for earth / for eh heaven

. . . .
. . . .
. . . .
. . . . in pain
. . . .

. . . . cuicatl . . . to h . . ear & that I found to be too much
& blessing / & my tale I sing

. . . . *married love* . . . . . / . . . .—*zme* . . . .
married love w/ pillow . . . .
w/ pillows for head & feet . . . .
. . . . *married love w/ pillow*
/ . . . . *quarrel*
. . . . *husbond & wyf)*   [margin: *claro no me chingues*
pues]
. . . . *h* . . . .
. . . . *husbond & wyf*
violent quarrel btwn husbond & wyf
. . . . . . *husbond & wyf* . . . . *husbond & wyf*
one who causes disturbance btwn husbond & wyf—
. . . . . . *husbond & wyf woman w/ 6 bairn & a husbond & pillow* . . . .
man w/ lovers & their children [10] . . . .
. . . . *w/ roof-tree for their house*
. . . . / *house in which live 3 women* . . . *& 1 man*
two women w/ many . . . . *[13]*
. . . . *in their house w/ their husbonds*
. . . . *woman* . . . *w/ child* . . . . *¿ ?* . . . .
& 2 women on each side of house—each w/ child
. . . .
2 women who live in same house . . . .
PALAVER each time they . . . .
& 3rd woman enters door
. . . . *& man comes to woman who has husbond*
& . . . .
requests . . . . *live w/ him*
/ *3 men* . . . . *her* . . . *me* . . . . *good god good good god* . . . .

adultery w/ a woman who lives
. . . . *her husband*

wyf bathes in river
. . . . *watches to see that no one shoots her* . . .
fire /
ardent love

b

ORIGIN: legit copy / MS 22954c-8 Engraved stone second draft / Mid-late November 1989

From out Mot there came one bigass egg. Sd Egg broke in half

& there have ye heaven &earth

& I "quotato" here in detail:

> *Now Hesiod reflects some of this in his still mythic cosmology / for out of Chaos (which he says wuz mist & darkness) wuz begotten Erbos & Night as well as Eros or Desire & also death. You will note / therefore / that w!hat [sic] we now see by centering again   ordered-question away from Kosmos back to man as source of his own sense & act of order / that displaced element in old cosmology wuz not desire but previous term of it / physical enjoyment. PHYSICAL ENJOYMENT—& here perceptions of our ancients extremely subtle—identified w/ chaos itself / boss / & only out of its jointure w/ spirit cd desire come.*

& out of death—

[1522]

MS 60666c-6 / *Codice Mojaodicus* 44:79 / corrected typescript sent to
Marina / signed & dated 15 November / along w/ typescript Marina
includes notes for Cortés in order to explicate passage references / clearly a
propaganda piece intended to glorify the Spaniards who pose as chosen
Xian Yoropeon
natural superiors to all indigenous Messomurkans / as old world to new
& various distorted reflections

CANTO FLORIDA
—UKASA—
XOCHICUICATL

"to be CAXTILLAN"

first conquer first-world conquistador:

Hernan our conqueror hero sez:
"he recibido piropos como bizpocho / papacito / neenyo lindo y cosas asee /
"la verdad es que el pueblo estAh ciega /

"soy I'm so intrEPido / un guerrero Yoropayo / bueno: es bien
"importante que tu condiclOn FIsika estAY bien / bueno:
"estoy pendiente de esas cositas cabrOna"

bueno: ¿ye treat yr women like a real old Mezkin do ye? ¿& how? digo:

"I'm un hombre who yearns for my soul's sensual fulfillment senyora / I'm
not a "man w/o belief in abnegation of bloodrushing desires / so deep my
desire & muy "much of wine
"& song / all that yea / donya . . ."

SUCH prophecies spouting from Chapultepec spring
            & them dudes from distant lands / sunriseward
perfect   [added by Cortés in margin]
            palefaced caballeros of the Quixtiano faith

who perfected products & services   [margin: *interpolation*]
changed & exchanged at everfaster
rates / & w/ knowledge to design
& create value efficiently
market it effectively
& to be becomingly true

w/ their markets conquering Amurka
simultaneously making & imagining Amurka
& w/ Amurka depending so on those trade markets why clear to see that

¡yes! ¡their gods were good!

& Amurka's gods just another sacrifice for their better gods appeasement just another sacrifice not even their gods' greatest or ultimate sacrifice / chingao

    [Cortés crosses several lines here dealing w/ ritualistic human sacrifice &
    flower warfare]

    —now that's some logos over mythos & so many now
    manipulated & marginalized signs
        & not stories of Amurka but stories of Amurkas
    & not Amurkans but Amurkans faberized fables
    down to this then / yes down to this then
    one official argument sung legitimate
    draped all over this newest transatlantic world:

    one quadrant of the esphere   [margin: *interpolation*]
    found fortune / another fell close /
    & the other two squares
    secluded & determined
    themselves thousands of years
    behind   in terms of
    technology / literacy /
    necessary political organization
    infrastructure/ economic development
    defense / machinery & discipline [¡ !]

    entire realms of machinery manufacturing
    goods & elites from nons—that distinction

    from focusing close as possible
    to zeroes w/o falling in the pit & everyone
    has its place specialized & hierarchized & reproduced

    but listen our conquistador: "jus' 'cause it can happen that everyone at some
    time "fries a couple of eggs or sews up a tear in a jacket/ we do not
    necessarily say that "everyone is a cook or a tailor ¿do we?"

    [¿ ?] & further adds:

    "two greatest
    "inventions of the human
    "mind are writing
    "& money—the common
    "language of intelligence
    "& the common language
    "of self-interest."

    & yes a conquestor like Hernand Curtez [sic] to whom conquest
        of knowledge went also w/ conquest
        of power—& of markets &

    he axed his Mexcan [sic] audience what their
        preferred genre—¿myth or argumentation?

"WE WANT MYTH malinche: quieremos los meethos malinxe"
via
   Marina
& "WE WANT NARRATIVE claro que HELL YES" & lit copal singing
           "ohuaya
           "ohuaya
           "y ahua yya o ahua yia yiaa
           "ohuaya ohuaya"
fine:
& so to forge
La Conciencia ($) de La RAZtlána ($)($) in the smithy of nuestra alma

SO Cortés blessedly axed his lady
that bien firme ruca / la vieja de compa Chuy for inspiration
& born from this side of his white noggin he rolls out w/ :
"here's one myth fer ye brownies: yes / Amurka existed / awaiting
"her blessed Yoropeon conquerors / patiently waiting
"& waxing primitive waiting / waaaaaaiteeeng / & so generous Yorope
"shared its vast & better knowledge to fill Amurka's
"deficiency in knowledge & grant Amurka HUMANITY / yes Amurka
"patiently waiting for centuries to reveal
"itself to that first Yoropeon who came
"to touch her caress her / seduce her & to . . ."

        ¡BANG!   ¡BANG!   ¡BANG!

                        ¡vamanos!
                        ¡vamanos güey!

right that's abrupt: but consider &
fancy that fancy trajectorized cultural myth product
Hispano ($) hat worn shorn
        & those torn brown britches & SING:

Non. Faber is sapiens too
not a secret / no / & you've not

done either try them Meester Conqueror. But a quarter
really hadn't got there yr kind say w/o
reading—they say—como dicen—yet but looked at language
as image or a certain combination
of writing w/ the what folks
wd sometimes call archetypal symbols
tho w/o alphabets included
going straight from eyeball to brain
w/o verbs spelled out for one's eye
to make yr own image based on yr
knowledge of images gathered

for however long . . . generations / whole statements
of picture arithmetic & letter
& still all beside the point

read these fruits of yr own
tyrannical labor:

& here I must stop here I must further interject / the poet writes & here I write this
b/c so much propaganda makes me feel stinky:

Carajo: nay / read this sr. Conquistador CABRÓN:

> *We are a product of 500 years of struggle: first against slavery /*
> *then during the War of Independence against ethSpain / then to avoid being*
> *absorbed by North Amurkan imperialism / then to promulgate our*
> *constitution & expel the Phrench empire from our soil / later the*
> *dictatorship of Porfirio DiAZtlán denied us the just application of the*
> *Reform laws & the people rebelled & leaders like Villa & Zapata emerged /*
> *pobres / just like us . . .*
>
> *We've been denied by our rulers the most elemental conditions*
> *of life / so they can use us as cannon fodder & pillage the wealth of our*
> *country / they don't care that we have nothing / absolutely nothing / not*
> *even a roof over hour heads / no land / no work / no health care / no food or*
> *education / nor are we able to freely & democratically elect our political*
> *representatives / nor is there independence from foreigners / nor is there*
> *peace or justice for ourselves & our children . . .*

Thanky Lacandon /
hindsight 20/20 but history never stops—

& their demise those here first for all everyone knows
their demise patterned under Aztec / Spanish / Mexican / Texan
Dutch / French / British / Russian / & Amurkan chains
& these Amurkas bathed always in blood
& history always aware / we can sense /
but we sense ourselves seeing history surround us
into powerlessness

& our conquistador replies:
"clearly yr inferiority complex implanted
"this second-half of this previous century
"chingao"

& our poet w/ history before him / yeah & the accumulation of riches
& death technology for Amurka worldwide after him responds
didn't much help much of this world
from wanting freedom / defined
as nearing Amurkan geopolitical voice & dependent authoritarian regimes
built from material defects of freedoms

one spiraling vortex of doom wrapped in a flour tortilla mass-produced

arepas

(arepas 'coz this ain't just one Messican discourse of course)

gringo yanqui: for in one free society
such as we own policy's bound to fail
which deliberately & obscenely violates our pledges
& principles & treaties & our rule of law & that's conquest's spirt hombre

that's our Amurkan conscience friend & that's
a reality

makes ineffectual an unAmurkan policy
& in all Amurka's historic struggles
Amurka finds its strength in developing
& applying its principles

yeah / like Yoonaited Estaits wd
permit . . . herida abierta indeed—
guácala great white conqueror ye make my retch—

"hey hey easy now" sez Cortés "take it easy"

& Cortés: "yr literal god adamnic language too
"poetik yr imaginative literalism yes senyor
"we have here one imaginative variety of writing
"relating in ambiguous ways toward truth & beauty
"pues: knowl/wedge
"& as anyone w/ half an Yoropeon brain (& other half who cares
"cd tell ye 'ye can't have art w/o resistance in yr materials'"

seaMOAN: hell that's one foul rag & bone shop in yr heart amigo
& yet but rather one finely tuned BROWN MACHINE
composting [sic] by field
& yes it's mostly this: language ain't something to be understood . . .
it's something to be carried out
up above: sun / ugly infected sore

[pagination resumes after several damaged pages / the following
handwritten portion inserted]

& finally Hernan sez

"problem is bubba / too much Messkins & not 'nough
"Amurkan courage / not 'nough Amurka here /
"hell then le's go on & make this Amurkan move
"it beaner
"or greaser / "

"mil desculpas" sd some Mexicanos to these greedy

greeng@s / conquerors / paisan@s
"this is our land senyorde—"

—"call me great white lord Nando" sez Curtez [sic]
"& lemme borrow yr daughter for a spell & I might

"let ye work fer me
        "meedhar Payo:
    "ye'll use those dimes I pay ye to unscrew some things round here
    "& yr pockets & cupped hands to fetch water from muh well"

& Payo—er / pardon—Felipe Contenís sez "¿eres unos de los White Hispanics
            "o one of dose Hispanic Hispanics who can boss me round
            "pocho patón? I—"

[end of handwritten portion / typed manuscript resumes]

    "it's this: OPERATION 'YNDIAN SHIELD'
    "leaving field wide open for sufficient
    "& well satisfied monstrous appetites
    "for this mission in Xst for Xst as my
    "bridge to gold & slave women & land
    "& by my faith these heathens will learn
    "of our truest trust in our lord Chuy Xst
    "in all our suns & all everafter &/or before"

    & all burned: [the following composed in glyphs]

    god   mouth
    country
              mountainwind   locality
one man

                    perdón: person   wood   plant
    tree
                            place   fish   &
              dress too

    DA   /   DA   /   GA   /   KHA
    KA   /   QA   /   la   /   MA
    NA   /   PA   /   RA   /   SA
    sha   /   wa (we wi   wu
    ZA
    Lives
              Loved   in   Amurka

              footprints
              descending
              from heaven
                                                    feathers
                  jaguar   &
                                                    flower

              20 jaguars

all burned:
                                    red jewel
              fire serpent

turquoise fan

        jaguar
          torch   cobweb

          braided   plumed serpent
          w/
w/ jewels
          flints

all burned:

¡o O o O O O my Lord the Flayed One!

        Xipi Xipi rah rah RA

[1962 / 5th sun / our present]

MS 44765d-145 (Private Collection) / typescript signed by Francisco "Pancho" Chastitellez Sr / grandfather of Chaley Chastitellez / songs gathered in shoebox at Pancho's Tuxson barrio apartment / December:

Radio AZtlán Amp & Alternator airwaves / Gila Valley

SONG: TransHistoricoOntological Honkey Tonk Blues

". . . an empty bottle / a broken heart
"& ye're still on mah mind"

goddamnit San Avabiche / hijo de la chingada a su puta madre turn up that radio goddamnit I love this one—

"yes: me vale verga all this mess:

"& bueno: mahs:
"alone & forsaken
"so blue I cd die
"I jes set here drankin
"til that bottle run dry
"to tryn forget ye
"I've turned to th wine

"an empty bottle / a broken heart
"& ye're still on mah mind"

S T R U M [sic]

"sd an emptyempty bottle & mah broken heart
"& yeee're still on mah mmmind"

spoken voice over music / & strummin strumm strummin

"w/ a little devotion now / steady: GO
"casul day like any other
"jet aircraft rippin a noisy sky
"& I sd to ye goodbye ye cruwel
"cruwellll girl ye've scorned this
"delicate boy ye've murdered
"somein truly fine wit-in im
"dulled im completely & left
"im alone in a dumb dilemma
"w/ his martini before im
"& another jet screaming
"more in some future imperfect later
"yes smart as ye somethin rare
"indeed some true pillar
"of sun rightly so rightly so"

up S T R U M M   órale thas um charp chit

"singin ever since those Greeks
"found earth a spherical body
"found emselves preoccupied
"by determinin its size
"& a calculatin its circumference
"smartly & blessdly from Zoos
"what they reached stonishinly
"accurate considerin their means
"& methods vailable tecknilogically
"then / / / WELL"

strum strummm strum strummm

"well when I fin mahself here
"spendin mah last dime getting drunker
"all the time & ye know ye just caint
"forget yr western civilizaaaaation
"& gods bless ye Yoropayin baby I love ye
"& I miss ye & yr amakin this Amurkan boy cry"

applause somewhere / yea get along li'l doggy hoppalong /
clear on thru clear on thru li'l lugnut alright alrighty turn
that down now pinches cabrónes get ta work en chinga pues

[2000 / 5th sun / our present]

MS 850312-49 / duplicate carbon copy w/ corrections handwritten by
amanuensis / some satirical verses over Chaley's ethnic leap / too scurrilous
for me to print here / but so you know / he actually wrote on the top margin
of the first page of the manuscript *you shd remember that leap which ye
took from that bridge* / but I will dwell no more on this delicate subject

Thusly: b/c somewhere realized—probably despues de
reading Bourdieu . . . no make that Fanon . . .
his danger of losing his life BECOMING lost to his / Mezkin people
/ in abstracted senseless senses / hotheaded & angry relentlessly
determined to destroy himself & also to renew contact
w/ those oldest leyendas most precolonial lifesprings
/ thanky Alurista he sd in his brains /
thanky to ye too Sr. Paredes—ah yes & Santa Gloria Anzaldúa
our Lady of Amurka wrapped in her red / white / bluegreen rebozo

BUT Pocho ye're más WASPy más gabacho que most gringos
Eso. Claro. Pues . . . ni modo—

'twas then our poet Chaley Chastitellez became Chicano . . . perdón/ ¡
Xicano⁴⁸ ! / ese hombre became Xaley Xastitellez/ revolutionary
(simpleton) /
yet his socalled artistic exigency concerned dynamics of his becoming
culture / defining sd culture / definition w/ respect to Méjico
& EE.UU. . . . ni modo—Xaley cd never
escape his gringitas after all he had

NO right / sin derecho / this Xicano cdnt even speak la lengua
     & he tried to sing Corky's song but his voice shook
     when Spanish inflected him gringostruck /
     esp b/c he cdnt roll his errrrrrrre:
       O . . . ¡LAZTLÁNARUS!
        ¡GRINgo penDEjo!
        !PINche paTON!
        ¡Possssho!
        ¡Caca-noso!
        ¡Cristalino caca cara e pan
         cruuuudo!
         ¡Blablablablancanieves!
         ¡Gagagachupín!
      ¡Quothe Sr. Quota! en Espanglish
      er whatever he called himself
  still he looked selfsame as truth's reckon & he felt some supposed sameness
cried & sang his songs w/ soundest sense / immense rhythms gained from Joyce / & he
sd

YO SOY AM I—no: that's SOY YO & yeah am amassed masses of mi

gente en de unaited esaites or meheeko afweda

---

⁴⁸ Xicano / eh *X*icano / ¡Now what the DEFFIL can that mean!

& & & & . . . yeah / I've been absorbed—comfortable
disease—puro asimila'o / tigre del norte

MEZKIN-AMURKAN

hijo del sol y de la mañana y de la chingada / illegit Sunkid—yeah son of
kid father for my ol' man—órale
& his heart jumped when arcoiris split his almond eyes
      but then instantly:
LOOK: yonder bald eagle swooping down upon aguila morena w/ snake in
its
clutches

            YEAH this eagle's for ye Xaley puro gringo /Spain
stains on yr
      whiteskin /
            claro . . . green GO . . . to Méjico
& pack yr Xicano neoindigenous essentialist[49] false consciousness
           ugh / & go / GO / veteverde / GO
       go see greengo & understand
       when all's sd & done: history culminates in US
          ¡ holy telos !
          ¡ jumping ghost of Wakeen Mierdieta !
     GO to Mexico greengo go

       decorations w/ flowers & sawdust / music / fireworks
       loud pops each night sometimes early morning
   certainly not gunshots Mexicans will assure ye greengo
       ye're perfectly drunk if you think those gunshots
       & what ye'll expect from yr research
       & yr poetic intelligence:

---

[49] Xicano neoindegenous essentialism—ugh—& no he wd not sport his brown beret / mind / but rather his Sinaloan
Stetson—yes—it's quite accidental that he wuz born Amurkan—but / after all / Amurka IZ eternal

indigenous magic / catholic religion / capitalist technology

& Chaley—sorry/ Xaley / stops to think—

[end of typed manuscript / handwritten on back of sheet the
following / handwriting not that of amanuensis]

> *HERS: small boxed corn kernels*
> *& writes in his notes*

MAYHAP FOURPART STRUCTURE:
1) PSYCHOSEXUAL/
2) ETHNOPOLITICAL/
3) SOCIOECONOMIC/
4) PHENOMENOPHILOSOPHICAL/

[the following written in amanuensis's hand]

ADD HARE COSMOVISION
RAVEN POME FROM AK VISTA DAY
NORTHWEST NATIVE MYTHS
TECHNICIANS OF THE SACRED
DIA DE LOS MUERTOS
CHUPACABRA warriorpoet
DEC: VIRGEN DE GUADALUPE—eat the baby so as not to buy next cake
TURKEY Y MOLE
HISTORY OF PASOLE
REVISE SISTER REVOLUTION TO GUADALUPE
BELT BUCKLE HER FACE

[2008 / 5th sun / our present]

    & so Tío Pancho & Chaley
    penetrated Manhatitlán deep
    sloppy July humidity tangling
    them until 'Times Esquare'
    as Tío used to say
            tho he'd never been
    & so his Sinaloan destiny linked
    w/ web to this eastern place & so
            Chaley Chastitellez
            wd dump his Tío's
        ashes wherever he
            thought best here in Times Esquare

    Chaley looked down at his Tío's new shell / then sd
    pero oye listen oye
           & ¡ look ! Tío—LA LUZ / sd Chaley to his Tío
            whom he toted in black plastic sack
            cinched at top &
            . . . how long & hidden
            Tío in his dreams followed clinking cloud rolling
                curtains / gas green neon
                billowing / crowd furrowed /
                strange brows—

    SURE: mighty torrent / sure as its might / crowd /
    & calmate Tío—hush yr thunder sd Chaley clearly speaking his Tío
    —shun what's common & mean
            6,982,488 lights flashing fury thoughtbulbs & another
            6,982,488 & noise

    & his Tío from beyond: "para el tiempo to boot" & these lines:
    COSMOS black blanket star speckled planets / nebulae / constellations of
            Suns

    ¡ LEND YR EARS ! thought Chaley to the folks
                     exiting Planet Hollywood &
            to some beautiful fifty-foot tall pouty-lipped
            white young man or maybe woman O Tío

    away alone along on forty-two Chaley walking
    solo west w/ Tío's ashes in this sack / plastic /

    watchale / walking Tío's ashes north / past
    Swatch hugged sidewise O / servicio hear Tío
    here time's money Tío / Chaley sd to his uncle's ashes / sack cinched

    time y movement / in Ethiopia time metaphors / sd
    Chaley to his
    uncle's ashes / of movement don't exist WELL

            buckle no arrow

buckle no fleeting

y ¡ SENSE !

& Chaley Chastitellez reckoned here en Nueva Yor lights / lights & folks
  who
   ask C for money
     & ask say / b the b / ¿ wha'sin thet bag boss ?

  & / ¿ canna git some ?
  & C: no / es mi tío en esta bolsa

 ¡ BASTA !
 y know forever sus primos no tienen su papa not now nor forever Chaley
     & the body just disappears
       becomes dirt dirt dirt
  well his ashes anyway / never to have visited Times Esquare w/ blood
        mixed w/ his flesh

  O TÍO / dead / dead / dead / first blind as a bat in political matters
         racist / como Ezra Pound
  racist Tío / fearful Tío / hatred / hardhearted / contra women / Jews /
homosexuals / Puerto Ricans—evil Tío of different worlds really
     refracted bigtime ¿& he wanted Times Esquare?
     no manches:
       he'd die from selfhatred
selfpity selfdread
  all these lights Chaley looked up
    always electric day here in this place
    Chaley needed a dark place & he
      eyed a green flowerpot
      sweat in his eyes pot
  over yonder & sd to the box
  there are two things in this dirty dirty world
     up he looked at groups of students chaperoned
     by workingclass folk from Wax Museum / J-LO
  second: visible thru the window: two things: brute facts & social facts
  Tío: brute facts exist w/o man Chaley still speaking to cinched bag:
     but objex in relation to time: after the lantern yard

loss of God
  (absence of meaning & Chaley speaking faster
   / rambling:
     raveloe: space w/o time . . .
       repetition instead
      cyclical time HALLO QUETZALCOATL
      I order ye universe / TIMES SQUARE
   ¡ zsTOP !
      & nothing / nothing

  look Tío: here he spoke to the ashes in the box:

shells.

[2021]

MS 588800-1 paper

GLYPH:

[page]
[1848 misc suns]

for weak & fed Messicans cd not resist them Amurkans
since them Messicans wanted nothing in this world
as ferociously as los Amurkanos wanted that land
jus like Yorope finishin Yorope's business ye cd sey

[page]
[1521 misc suns / trans]

then immediately upon morning commanded / ordered
our Captain Cortés to make / perform alone / one / only
golden cross on there same / like likeness / appearance who / which on
heaven so / thus splendidly / gloriously shining saw
& he before him [to] carry / bring / bear commanded again & also to make
one mama for all to love forget yr Huitzilobos
then those heathens as soon as them on that holy sign of the cross beheld
then happened they immediately took fright / terrified / affright & to flee
turned
& Curtez [sic] glorious Xian conqueror then victory had & his army / troops
those heathens slew / destroyed verily & he also / in addition / some there
on that lake / drowned / immersed
as they chased them / & as the famous / illustrious / glorious Cuahtemoc
again / afterward / thereupon home returned to his own stronghold into
Tlatelolco then commanded Emperor Temo to send for / summon all elders
& scholarly knowers of Aztec folks'
                       [folces genetive singular—¿folks' or folk's?]
wisdom
& asked he them whose sign / token that be might which he on from heaven
so gloriously shined saw they then sd: "It is that great heavenly sign to
which the "living God's son upon suffered."
O shit / he sd
then: my soul's v. sad & will be till that
day when Cortes gives us back gold & gods
he's hidden away /

[page]
[2002 misc suns]

C wore his favorite deerskin t-shirt: an image
of a featherplumed gringo
wearing one bigass gold medallion
& a velvet cloak trimmed in gold
& text: Brothers & Comrades

Let Us Follow the Sign of the Holy
X in True Faith / for Under
This Sign We Shall Conquer . . .

& in his obsidian mirror sd to self:

. . . setting sail next day . . .
                    I'm yr
                    Humble servant

[page]
[1522 misc suns: trans]

[Cuahtemoc according to one history /
one *glyph* / pardon this translation b/c I spick glyph muy feo
bien feo:]

*& as he stepped away he noticed clouds ripping into sky between pyramids
clouds extending across three states & into ocean on either side these
clouds like his whole symbolic dimension of everyday lived thought & life
now his common ritual of disinterest & general unrest & again to old
routines & attachments sweet metanoia clean spirit alas / toasts to
countless simultaneous conversions mutually reinforcing & supporting one
another / to transformations of view he HAD now again HAS of
socialsymbol relations this life Temo this is yr life is thiiiiis my life on my fly
yes yes this empire on yr life this is yr life these choices ye made / joder /
chido Temo open up yr eyes & done: & remember They asked him ¿what
religion[50] do y' think y're? & he responded: claro puro Azteco what ye
think chingao / I mean look at these short legs dudes / & They sd w/ white
thunder which They struck down deep into his bones deeper into his blood
that YES Y'RE Mexica [blink] & Temo shook but didn't know what
happened & so left*
*that steep temple & on the way out stopped an old man selling cocitos &
bought one single scoop & as he strolled away he took Their
Pronouncements & lived his life accordingly: emperor school / omens /
sacrificial symbolic descents / Work Leisure Stylizations of his life spoken
for in advance & They watching from on high from Their stone mansions on
the hill overlooking ocean bluewhite rocky beaches lowtide green rockcliffs
good place to nap shd ye find yrself on those forbidden trails where They
walk Their dogs & servants when They break to dream up different classes
of determinisms for all They keep occupied* [end]

[page]
[2004]
& glyph:

> *as Chaley holding Tío in his plastic bag w/ strap*
> *holding past / can't / product / & produce*
> */ movement on / SPACE   / now only exists*

---

[50] understood it derives its essential impetus from its answers to existential questions abt conscious human
conditions & life's meaning / its explanation of historical origins / natural order / contemporary events / its power to
impart by affording true knowledge of whats governs this world as universe

H   O   W
mechanical time sustains struggle
        T   O
C   H   E   A   T
                T   I   M   E
there's a sick science of finding objectivities in culture /
extracting art ART
                art's way of finding artfulness of objex
                / & yet / & Y E T : Tío Pancho w/ lifegiving brain
never reckoned labour as even / minimally / part of his life / /
/ /   rather: sacrifice / of his life / life began he sd
after work at cantinas in Brewery Gulch / BISBEE / AZtlán
                at table / public house / yes / in bed w/ rented rucas

                & W/ THESE ASHES MIXED W/ LIFE HE THREW
HIMSELF INTO PLAY OF
                        WORLD / & DANCED W/ IT

                venerable aging man / scoured hands
                —cut from wood   today again
                memory of Tío Francisco Chastitellez
                framing sidewalks for others to walk on
                see these feet lacing tennies Tío
                / to walk across / pulling grass w/ our hands
                sun & water

                TIMES E$QUARE CAPITALI$T AIR

                & tedium of shingling causes me this witness
                all of this

[good glyphy good yes / easier to see cuts there
[& finally this one: page]

[1521 misc suns]

but before I can accept these ladies
Cortés sd to his Tlascalan listeners & become yr brother
ye all must abandon yr idols which ye mistakingly
believe in w/ all those hearts ye rip out still
beating beating / abandon those wicked devils
ye think gods & sacrifice no more hearts
& when I see that done & all yr heathen sacrifices
at an end / our brotherhood cd be that much firmer
but the girls he added must become Xians before
I can receive them & you people must all
give up sodomy / for I see here standing before

me boys dressed as women who practice
this accursed vice for profits & here at yr temples
this day ere day dawns make it so . . .

& brothers us all we shall be
& we'll save you from yrselves

[page]
[1915 misc suns]

Chaley's abuelo Pancho Chastitellez Sr de Sinaloa sent to President Wilson
a piece of chicken liver
three pieces of prized chicken fat
& a poblano chili wrapped in red paper

this means war President Wilson sd softly to himself

[page]
[1531 misc suns]

Huichilobos & Tezcatlipocita intend to leave
this forsaken Mexican desert[51]
& once again native gods leave Mexico
& Yropean ones enter to take their places . . .
¿what's the significance of that?
¿& where do they go?
well Xochimilco for one— [manuscript ends here]

---

[51] instant reminder: revolutionary Xaley camping in desert island Dos Cabezas west of Willcox / AZtlán / for one week walkin 'round / deserted ol' land / & some body there / covered w/ dirt & gravel / only thing showin: feet / so he called some older tribesman & one dug out this corpse & said "damn kid wasn't even twenty by the look of his jaw" / broken nose / teeth missing / blue flannel coat / no pants / "probly dead for bout couple days" / no smell / & off hear that piano / & further guitar S T R U M for here wd be some song / & they drove into Willcox called the cops & those tribesmen made cross signs across their torsos / & they set up camp at the Motel Seis / & the tribesmen passed around a handle of Old Crow / & they finished it / & Xaley never got one drink / & as they passed out Xaley stared at ceiling / ¿is this desert land crazy? asked Xaley / ¿do folks die for fun?   S O L O   S T R U M destructive desert /

[2010 / 5th sun / our present]

> transcription from chapter xi of the *Codice Mojaodicus* /
> Amatl paper screenfold fragment painted both sides

G L Y P H:
IN magneefico Makesicken Arizone ye begin again
                every single day
porque en Mayheekan Arizone's wild wild west—
                & as some wd AZtlán—
        those real machos get born hourly to die cabrón

(& yes to cross & get bagged in hate . . . but for that wait)

& look now then we have this one / one more macho
que Jorge Negrete yes it's true . . .
but PERame charro / this sometime macho progenitor /
w/ legendary huevos the size of oxen / homredes verdades

(but really un chaquetero known to cuello
al gonso just abt every day of any week / a regular maraquero
& no stranger at all to polishing el palo)

& say this to yrself Chastitellez / vaquero / snap
that yolked plaid shirt &
¡OYE! make play vaquero barero:

& lock strong that song & so make me sicken
w/ yr stinky geetar & play it nicelike & make
me smile / ¿wd ye? / & give me strength to sing
                yr honkytonk song wey /

for ye damnwell know yaint ever gonna let yr imag-nation
                outgrow this ere damn rodyo:

now sit ye down & listen up: heah:

[page]

S I N G:
look / hoss / see him there cross
that dusted yellow creosote dandyin prissy
& as he sloshes his Sinaloan sombrero
at a jackduce angle over his off ear—
his spurs catch sun's glint
/ shine naked as a brandin iron
since he swaggers to all dressed up like a sore wrist
lookin like a dime novel on a spree /
sportin one of them black suits what w/ no front
& jus a lil windbreak down on back
& redsilk neckerchief over one sorry fringed buckskin shirt

& them sealskin chaparajos & ridgid yella ostrichflesh boots

sho nuff made thisun look
like a reglar ole mail order catalog a la chingada—
puro vaquero nortanyo able to face any electric slide or achy breaky corazón
/ this cowboy livin la vida cruda . . .
for we cd smell him before he stepped in
rancid w/ that brindled taste in his hot mouth
/ a fullgrowed case of booze blind
breath near strong nough to crack a mirror
from hoochin that trantula juice strong nough
to draw bloodblisters on a rawhide boot yesterdiddy
& deep into yesternitey
sippin silverbullets & wildcat in mexkeet tree shade
all daylight for some seven hours
& after sunset he bowlegged it on over to yonder honkytonk
after kickin a few cars & nappin in a bank parking lot
to inoculate hisself another nine in nightdark
& to nurse himself from all the multiplicities of snakebite
& after stumblin back cured to the rancho mostly drunkern a biled owl
& hell if ever seen borrach'd blind
he woke roadside
jes norte of Triple-T restaurant & gas
face covered w/ ants red throbbing skin
next to a yucca & barbed wire
& lo a headache so big
it wouldnt fit into a hoss corral
/ yea he done woke up cussin in his brains w/ his head
feelin big nough to eat hay w/ hosses in Montana—
& he stood his best / crawled himself up
dusted himself off / opened & shut his eyes
& he sd to himself "chingao"
as he spotted his sombrero atop
the arm of a translplanted twelvefoot saguaro

"he looka lil somethin like a wd be Hay-soos Malverday
"w/ them ostrich boots all charroed up to the nines
"but w/ less sense nough to spit downwind" sez este wey
saloon patron number Juan

     & as he steps further into this bar w/ reclaimed
     flamingo-feathered sombrero tilted
     still eyes take him in
& as he bowlegs it on up
b/c they know provokin tipsy poetlikes as more dangerous
     than kickin a loaded polecat
      they sey nothing

what again w/ those yella cowboy boots clacking on cobble stones
& he wobblin on over direct from jes norte of Triple-T restaurant & gas
straight into here death's rodeo:
& let be known in this saloon

one's structure of time
gets recursive b/c Chaley Chastitellez had been on in heah before now

& right on thru them swangin doors he
steps for maybe the ninehundreth time in his life
in both Messica & Amurka & right now
between both in AZtlán
straight on thru into dusty borderland sunlight
stomach wrenching
& he: damn curse & recursivity cursed
cursed & he thinks
/ *& of all the cantinas in this wide wide AZtlán—*

b/c this güey steps into this Juan / this Juan w/ pockedface potholes
cacarizoed more profound than Grande Cañón
& squarish eye w/ even squarer pupil—prominent
roman nose / & the central incisors of his upperjaw
filed to shape squat stones & fangs projecting
from his mouth's corners / what ye might call
on the boundaries of humanity—
a reglar bucknun for looks
& biggern carajo como el pinche Machete—
cdn't hide no more than a hill—
& pobre Chaley fellin into
death's cantina here in Gila Bend / AZtlán
a town where most doors swing both ways
& so tough all the hoot-owls sing bass . . .
of sun / sand / sand / sun / & blisters & scarred heat
nough to addle the ol thinkerbox into a ruckus of apparitions
& here at the prophetically ominous & ordinary
Cantina Aqui Stoy Sperando / another temple
of Messican virility most especially so / & Chaley (again) bien pedo:
still lit up like a honkytonk on a Satdiddy nite
as he in fact had honkytonked for some nine
hours last night / Saturdiddy Norteño Nite
at Club Estadio Escandaloso on south sixth
in Tujxon there w/ imagination sufficient
to sculpt shapes of bottles tipped his way
many many times & each colder than the last . . .
& Chaley now—pues—not
zactly lookin like first prize at a bullshow
but w/ Xicano spur rowels as big as soup plates
stumbles in spittin pretty something abt
"ni mahs ni maynos de tres"
& "para todo mal mescal"
& receiving no response from that bartender
w/ waxed staches lookin like a monocled albondiga con pies
who continues to wax
a pintglass C asks in reaffirmed tone:
"OYE ¿hablas Chinglish wey or no?"

jukebox: . . . *singin she was Mex & I a Green-Go & so it cd not be* . . .

no response: & Chaley knows bad things wd be a-goin down
¿what in thirteen heaven is this? Chaley thinks

"¿what in thirteen heaven is this?" Chaley asks
& as he does—hiccup—so his identity thickens for:

jukebox: S   T   R   U   M   M   M   M   M—

> *. . . cuz she loved me in Messican & I truly loved her all in Green*
> *& I'm a-singin to you stranger*
> *she was Mex & I a Green-Go & so it cd not be . . .*
> *&c &c—*

"lissen here citizens" sez C
"hear that song I got something to sey abt that"

good / Albondiga: "¿whatchu wan hombre?"

"—me first—" sez this size nine Juan Juan
"—me first vaquero fore ye tread offense
"for this selection I chose on its merits of truth & beauty
"& generally painting chronotopically all I migt cd know
"spatially & temporally
"& what I know
"of a universal condition of humanity but before that
 "first to let be known I identify w/ this song first & foremost b/c
"Anglish equals the bedrock of this nation cum civilization son

"& that feller singin's communicatin
"w/ me / & his lady / abt miscommunicatin w/ same sd lady
"lordy I tell you what: that feller's singin abt singing
"& in so in Anglish / & tha's all I needs so looky here patnuh:
"best ye abt to talk to me in Anglish & not spoilen this song
"& listen / come join me
"as well ye know we's a-speakin sho Pochisme heah—
"hell beaner is as beaner does / de verdhas beanbag /
"& this feller's wd be vieja stayed in Messico
"to work the mocojate & grill Sinaloan chicken
"so my msg here's spiccin to me in anything but Arizone Anglish'd
"be bout as useless
"as settin a milk bucket under a bull—
"where I draw this from at this moment's my
"business compardre / coming from some deep border stuff / hear me
"& espeak like me for spiccin correct means
"yr livelihood & that of yr children . . .
 "ergo: in our bedrock of our Amurkan nationhood wey / eSPEAK
"Amurkan—& only Amurkan / in this desert of the ol A-Z
"this country unto itself / espeak Amurkan loud w/ Amurkan air
"pumping those lungs proudly espeakin Amurkan lib-ty
"love / godbless / & another thing ye know—
"in this cantina espeak only Amurkan
"& don't get started w/ language further buddy

"cause I know yr poetlikes stinks
"cabrón for . . ."

"—let me speak of love good sir" & Chaley pulls up
a nice seat hmm & Albondiga slides
a tumbler of rocky tequila strong nough to kill a goat
& make its hair stay stiff days after death
C's way / & C: say: "escuchen weyes:"

Jukebox: S T R U M S T R U M S T R U M /

don't be fraid of what ye learn
    reg'lar Meskin anchel she was
    & I a PEENshay GreenGo caBRONE
    & so & so & so (&c)
    our amore cdn't be—

"now ye hear that" nods "this trumps
"that small stuff compadray cuz poets know matters
"of the heart no conosen tongues: bwayno"
            —hiccup—
"perdon: well how universal you can judge:
"she left me all this dough & she from down yonder
"someplace w/o air conditioners
"hot / dry / unpaved roads & where folks
"wear war-achays & live w/ chickens inside
"their adobe homes afraid of narcos"

"see es la verdad" sez Albondiga "el surrr"

"& she left me all this plata for me to make my life w/
"& I never thanked her b/c she died died died . . .
"cursed really b/c she loved this güey—"

juke: S   T   R   U   M   M   M   M

"—so I never really sd thanks or gudbai
"& she had me this mostly greensican er greenskin whatever
"she had me & I still caint figger why . . ."
            —hiccup—
"perdon: mild as sweet milk that's how I remember her
"& basicly doomed from the first
"& basicly I'm a-thinkin abt how to find her
"thru poetry & writing her & even
"now that she's dead brangin her back
"w/ me to Manhatitlán to live / but first I got to get to Vegas
"tha's right / Vegas
"but basicly I've really jus been drinkin evernight
"gettin so hammered caint even member my name
"& scribblin illegible junk on misc pieces
"of garbage—"

& juke: S   T   R   U   M
s t r u m
         S   T   R   U   M

NOW picture this Juan / that Juan right there
scoots out his chair spitoooooon dink
rubs his hairy jaw & makes like some yogi
as he gracefully adjusts his huevos & his wranglers

"meedha ombray: I picked that song cuz
"I wanted t' hear it ay & ye damn well spilled it
"so I reckoned ye owes me back my dime / ¿intyendez mendez?"

"¿yever killed anyone before? I didn't murder her
"& I don't think anyone murdered her
"I think she jus died / on account of that curse I mentioned . . .
"unending torture maximum & mainly metaphysical—
"tha's good gonna write that down" & he writes
that down—

" . . . "

"—up & died like all she'd ever sey was gracias a diosito all the time . . . & . . . &
"soy tu principe estás bajo mí sombra que ya
"nada te apene ni te dé amarguras . . . "
& Chaley pulls out a fifty dollar bill for Albondiga w/ orders
to serve Juan until he kills this paper /

"chingao hombre / she loved ye" sez Juan to C now Juan-to-Juan:
"oye tomate un Tecate para take away the pain hombre—
"& Albondiga digo: two icecold pulques for me—see hombre
"yo say it hurts"—fang glisten yellow—"lived mucho of em
"myself I did / out in Fort Huachuca & down into Naco Snornora [sic]
"had my own band of wolfpack & we'd
"some suerte w/ las muchachitas / slippin em shots
"of that famous Spanglish fly & always always—thanks Albondiga—
 "here's to Ome Tochtzin"—gulp gulp gulp gulp—pause—belch
"eh . . . yeah always heroically dodging
"Cupiditas / thas right hombre: drugs / sex / violence / & glory . . .
"see hombre livin that tender machista dream . . . alas
"but eventually yr heart gets shook & yr done & slack
"patnuh . . . ¡quihúbole! hardern tyin down a bubcat
"w/ a piece of strang than sey no to love hombre
"when ye love—whom ye love—why ye love—
"see hombre eso es . . . & you ye ought to thank yr dang luck
"since thissun left ye a fine handla lechuga"

he thinks abt another glass of wildcat then
& Chaley notices back behind Albondiga a coffee pot
big as a dippin vat & the good Juan
notices Chaey's eyes look like they got campfire smoke in em
& for that Juan Chaley seemin as unhappily anxious

as a drunken scalded pup dizzily lookin for a snowbank
& thinkin somethin continuous & desperate
& Chaley sez before another hiccup—hiccup—

"tender give me a can of wine para llevar porfa—

"I'm walkin out into that sun this morn . . . Felipe Cotenís"

"god bless ye stranger"
"¿kyen is este bway?"
"órale"
—hiccup—
"go / sale sale sale—"
"—do what I have to do to get er back . . . jus as I finish drinkin & smoking"

"strike me as a progressive cowboy compadre
"ye do / downright genrous & rough/tough wearin
"loud boots / snakebit / & ass kickin—
"or like my pappy used to sey: 'like that John Wayne buttpaper:
"'rough & tough & don't take no shit from nobody' / that's you
"wey"

& Chaley knows full well hell will be a glacier before sunny Juan will quit
& tips his jackduced & flamingo feathered hat to his comrades & pours
out that last bit in her name & seys under his breath
. a l i n . h . & . . l . n . h e & yup—

& finally jukebox: *¿why do ye drink?*
                            & ¿why do ye go smoke?
                            & ¿why must ye live out all those pomes that ye
wrote?
"órale"
"órale"
"óral—" hiccup "—e"

outside hotsun & wind in eyes since last & walkin
as crooked as a snake in a cactus patch
starin at sky & seeing nothing & crackin that can of winedark sweet
yes fast into poetry further into pure poetry Chaley wills
stumbles / & somebody's mongrel chucho comes up whining
& sniffin at Chaley / vete al diablo cabrón

. . . colorín colorado

CANTO FLORIDO / UKASA / XOCHICUICATL

transcription from chapter ix of the *Codice Mojaodicus* /
Amatl paper screenfold fragment painted both sides / Mar-May

Chaley to la Güera Guerrera:
    "ye hate me / y're needy / ye send me to the region of the dea—"

¡ Chichi(s) meca !   ¡ Chingao !

"yr truth missles
"chill this blood & this blood frozen solid" that sd not S U N G:

& then in unison w/ each hand dug deep into his pockets
retrieving one canto ripped in two choice slices
& uniting them C read
& sang as he read:

. . . *yyyyyy estaba tomando cerveza muy feliz*	[&&&&&& he wuz drinking beer muy happy]
con su primo tlacuilo	[w/ his cousin tlacuilo]
como muy guapo estaba	[like he wuz muy handsome]
y muy estudiado era	[& muy cultured]
muchas chicas mexicanas	[many mexican girls]
conquistarlo deseaban	[wished to conquer him]
pero cuando la calaca lo vio	[but when La Calaca saw him]
prendada de el quedo	[she fell in love w/ him]
pero por flaca y palida	[but tho skinny & pale]
Chaley ni la pelo	[Chaley didn´t see her]
La Morena y La Güera deseaban	[Browney & Whitey wanted]
a este galan conquistar	[to this gallant to conquer]
y por el se peleaban	[they fought by him]
pero La Pelona llego y les dijo	[but Death arrived & told them]
lo siento chicas	[so sorry girls]
pero conmigo se va ha quedar	[but he's goin home conmigo]

& & & & addressed his wounds
this lady La Lllorona stood & stared
—no me chinges Cihuacoatl—
& then she turned & stalked away
her heels clacked away

"don't go"

                    cue: crashed table dishes shattering into shards

"I'm shattered ye're my
"wyf tonite doll I love ye

"ye buy me all sorts of stuff

"ye're good people
"ye're my lining
"if ye leave ye leave
"this glove worn
"inside-out

"& that's real" Chaley sd

stopped clacks / heaved back / more tears
slower tempo then / remembered whispers
in kitchen / clumsy that
night / cracking fine
furniture / slacked crotches
ripped he wanted to pull
her close w/ fury rip her
gut her

clacks directly toward him
unexpected / bueno: facil
& as she stepped to him
her eyes ran black down
sides of her face hot
candlewax & tears

"—y're a stooped stupid shitface Chaley
"Chastitellez: y've made yr goddamned
"choice—go read yr
"Joyce books all
"day &
"play w/ yrself—that's all ye really want"
she sd

"hey now that's not true"

"—Y're one stupid shitface farteyez"

> cue: state of undress / bared midriff (carajo)
> bared thighs (órale)
> / bared shoulders (n'hombro)
> / bared feet (eso)
> visible cleavage (& here he touched his pantcrotch)

> cue: hair to her bare shders/ mayhap beyond / hell he
> cdn't remember
> / wetbody drip drippy drippp—white
> wetback he toweled

> closed eyez (eso & ESO)
> she caressed that banana
> / zzSTop Chaley—

> mouth in contact w/ object

reclined / legs spread / widely /

F   L   A   S   H

nine-year-old Chaley stuffing TV remote in his mouth just to see if he cd reach his furthest molars top & bottom simultaneously success w/o choking CC hadn't flossed back there probably ever & remote 'pon removal stunk something rank

CHALEY: YOU NASTY

"—Yre stabbing my heart w/ at least 60 rakes"

"sorry" sd CC but verily such is love's pain

"—Shitface / shitface"

CC sd "let me g-get ye something w/ ice"

"—I wont say no."

& off for some Swowza on ice
wow he sd to himself
¿did I tell her I'd use
that I won't say no
line before because I got
that from Perec & I've
wanted to use it for
suuuuuch a long time?

& upon returning on that sofa
she sat next to C as he
took down from his shelf
& read to her in English
his Perec w/o E & also
mentioned more books
but not the *Wake* b/c that she
had previously sd
cd never be read
not like her blessed
transatlantic romanticism
& her pinche Wordsworth

& as his finger led her thru
translated French Chaley's
natural nahual stalked around
this pair / & La Llorona sipped
her tequila / deep sips mind
& Chaley's nahual sprinkled

some magic & La Llorona's eyes
teared more / más mascara

down her rosey cheeks

& w/ this magic delicate bushels of her dangling
blood red coils artificially
fanning & whisking her demeanor cosmic
as radiances of swhirls smoke ascend
w/ these two opened book before them
& spotlight them red as blood curls spiral
& sex captured on paper
& back behind that sofa returned C's nahual

& here Y E S here she set down her glass
& verily allowed our assistant
to pull down her petticoat

& only she sez to herself

"my demon-lover yes I sey yes Yes"

when ¡LO!—at his foot / shoved under door
shoved by one v. tender brown mano—no
doubt / stuck w/ silver seal
representing some / man's helmeted
head—¿what the fu—& under
this conquistador's visage / some
scroll w/ device thus: PERVIAM RECTAM
—¿rectum? . . . "eso chingao" Chastitellez sd

"¿wha's that?"

"mmmmnothin: ¿more Swowza lady?"

thru blue flew his view into her eyes

"well no matter: & again" sniffle "I won't sey no"

"ándale"

"¿you need me tonight? I mean / ¿why ye think I've got this curve
"on my hip if not to steady myself? Chaley I'm steady: & ye sd ye need
"my love tonight
"tha's what ye sd Chaley ye need my love"

"o yeah" . . . ojos que no ven chorizón que no siente

    pero this vamprio norteño sd I need yr blood not yr love
    not yr time nor yr capital /
    yr blood pendeja yr blood

& as explanation: I inflict much pain upon myself in this stylization of life I lead / &
I'd best not to add any of this to you / stroke hair behind ear / see since Ye're the only

one who's ever believed in me—cdn't tell you why—& see if Ye're near me I will shit
all over ye / glass of ice water / no not ready Ye know just can't do this anymore
sd we'd always be together sd tha y-yu did

talking out my ass what you ¿want from me kid?
¿kid?
for the rhyme only
now y-y-yu cant even look at me look at me LOOK AT ME
I'd prefer not to my eyes makin tears
QUIT SPANKING THAT GODDAMNED HUEHUETL ASSHOLE
y-y-yu want me to hate y-yu but I wont though y-yu're destroying me
hues fluctuating
I gots to be a-spreading my irrational fears

whose lines his lines she never sat & never sd & this happened somewhere else &
either way I've a bad cough & I cdn't remember if I wanted to I sat gray sky outside
sunflowers & over yonder dandelions who lives there stood remember something about
yes suh she wore some gray dress he bought in Tuxson & probably boots & her eyes
shone blue in her park & her face had tiny holes & he cd peer thru them directly into
her deep deep & now his eyes watered but nothing else not even from the gut came
from this then down swelled his water even then he cdn't sob slob sobbiddle SUE her
face . . . shit now a good time to smoke as good a time as any inflict more pain upon
his body which he read somewhere wuz more or less a disposable rocket anyway
rocket think too much of the rocket he sd to no one in particular out loud & he lit his
lighter it sparked good image of saguaro pulled out his tobacco unleafed a paper dipped
a proper amount smoothed it down & clipped w finger tips fold not supposed to fold
pues & rolled twice licked rolled / smoothed he put his labor between his lips like to
put my labor between her lips he sd to himself as a nanny walked by the park & lit ate

& NOW niños:

that Great Amurkan Prophet / Patriot
w/ colors that ain't ever gonna run
bleedin stripes & stars
barbacoa'd redmeat eatin
freedom starlovin
pickup truck drivin
prophecies transnationally:
O Sr Citizen Henry w/ Borders
—Operator Gatekeeper himself—
our gendered Amurkan Citizen
from güey on Right
not waiting one Minute(man)
for questions abt all them "beaners"
makin babies & fillin
classrooms w/ their primitive
landgwedge & spickin of that
bringing in lice & vermin / & venereal diseases
from that land o' tortillas
& to grease OUR lovely Amurka
w/ fatty carnitas & slimey cornhusked meatcakes . . .
invading our pie-loven Amurka
them goddamned animals
livin in trailers w/ 65-70 aliens after all
& thus takin 'pon himself O Sr Citizen Henry
(pos w/ additional Patriots like himself)
always always always urged them brownie drones
on back yonder to their Queen Shakira
or whoever
back into that dysfunctional haven of narcos
& death they have always ran from

& O Sr Citizen Henry of impeccable
personified smoothness
& slender veiny whiteglove
encased hands
& enormous—nay—vast—cultural geometry
complex & awkwardly dignified
behind his paleface / one vast distinctly Amurkan
face between here & his historic formerly
reading to schoolkids
at Francisco Kino Elementary
in Tombstone / AZtlán turns
that next page in his newest picturebook
Down from Amurka / Back to Castizalandia
young reader version of his equally as childish
adult study *¿Who Are They? The Greasing of Amurka's National Identity*
invited by his teacher wife to read to these
chamacos / mostly brown in shape & texture
but Amurkan in location / & lookin
at him all settin there all brown & bigeyed

lookin up at Sr Citizen / I tell ye / ye'da
split yr Levi's & dropped bears
if ye'da seen it—
        lo que pasa es . . .

he held up that selfpublished picturebook
& ¡O racista Henry![52] read:

"& one day some beaner son of a shameless squah—"

[image of moustachioed Tío Taco]

"decides to try his
"luck against il reeyo bravo
"but first prays to his 'santo'
"some masked loochadoor wrassler named San Avabiche
"& after a-lightin four candles
"walks close
"on his dry Meskin land & he aint been
"away from this same spot for but two weeks
"& as he's wading w/ his black plastic sack
"containing his clothes & his cacahuates
"tortillas & energy drink some 'greengo' hero out
"of nowehere pops up in front of him"

[image of Uncy Sam w/ thick cristalino frontier pointed finger]

"'CHINGAO' sez that paylado con grasa

"& Sammy our Sammy that Amurkan hero
"who of course that Beaner wdn't know
"sez 'hey there Meester Moehaydo
"'hello aint seen you for a spell
"'¿where you been?'

"well this pepperbelly sez something in Messikin
"& Tío Sam sez somehow knowing
"that wet nodding yonder
"right / up on that theah dry land / tierra firma
"back on over the madreland"

[image: ¿now where's that? / dark wasteland contrasted with green lushness]

"'say compadray: ¿ain't it wet up there
"'on that dry land you descend from ameego?
"'¿zit coo & refreshin there?

---

[52] ¡O Henry! pues suck *this* tamale / cabrón / for YOU have greased all of US as one nation w/ yr tamalefear / ¡grasa a tu madre! / & soft Henry's soul appears suddenly & clears its throat / clinking chains / ahem / ahem / & offers that poetic Amurkan sensibility & that Carolina propriety: "shut yr mouth greaser / spic / taco choker / bean guzzler / wet / peon / spiggoty spic / dirtcaked paylado"
    yeah: not bad / good ghost guest & host & zás: gone / always w/ that last word / chingao

"'¿duz it have waves & ripples?
"'¿cain't ye sur-vive in it?'
"& just then his gabacho retired professor friend pops
"up too / some sunbird from up near Twin Cities
"his RV plugged in over under yonder mexquite
"reality court television shows talking justice
"& this fast-talkin gabacho / dedicating thirty days
"to defend Amurka like a true [sic->] pitriot
"sacrificing his own time to defend Amurka's desert
"wasteland border & this Dr Birote—"

[image: yanqui blowhard blofero sportin tweed blazer w/ elbowpatches]

"PhD sez:
"'this dry land ye descend from's imaginary Paco Taco / one completely non-existent
"'imaginary thing / nothing real at all' sez thisun
"'Makesicko makes this nation retch so swim on back
"'less ye want this leather Amurkan size 10 straight up yr coolo—'"

[image: size ten school-of-the-Amurka's-issued-red/white/blue combat boot]

er . . . ¿chingao? ¿quien es este güey?
one buki in the back calling the ghost of Cortés / Gregorio Cortés plees plees come
plees . . .

"'ahem' in unison kids"

"'so sorey seniores' as that cookaratcha crawls
"back to that shitpile he came from . . .
"here / let me hold this illustration high so y'all can see
"real nice what Messico looks like—"

[image: brown babies w/ bulging hunger bellies / & shacks walled w/ newspaper]

"¿now where was I? . . . ah—
"'that's right' sez Prof Birote to Uncy Sam
"'our duty our Amurkan duty
"'our neverendin battle to secure Amurka's borders
"'& to reveal to all the 3rd world Paco Takos those real aspects
"'of their putrid nations' inferiorities relative to Amurkan
"'wealth / sweetness / goodness / in our kind eyes shining so clear
"'& how dare ye challenge our national sovereignty
"'& rule of law/ brownies'"

[image: WALLS & WALLS & still more WALLS conrete WALLS & razorwire]

"& our Uncy Sam smugly & w/ outstretched hand

"shakes Prof Birote's extended ringed fingers & sez—
"lissen closely niños—he sez:
"'well They sey eternal vigilance is the price of liberty . . .
"'They sey that / & they sey this Amurka's Being in Time

"'this Amurkan chonotope's suffering from invasive
"'dirty beaners from down on southward luggin northward
"'babies / they try to anchor to this land spickin backward slangwedge /
"'& bringin over that plain ol inferior Indian blood . . . brown bastards /
"'kaysadilla-eatin / greasy-headed / filthy drugsmugglin
"'mules / got-damn . . . gotdamned freehelayros . . . '"

[image: la Sra Guadalupe w/ five soiled Chueys at her unsandaled feet]

"now lemme ask ye one question kiddies / & be honest
"lemme axe ye : ¿ how can an Amurka of 300,000,000
"absorb 100,000,000 poor / uneducated / Esthpanich
"spickin wets & still be Amurka? answer & axe yr padres
"that & see what they sey / got that smartypants—
"yeah / I'm talking to you in the back there w/ those
"Amurkan subsidized glasses there in the back / yeah TÚ
"quit cryin . . ."

y los niños: ". . . . ."

"I argue in my controversial ¿Who Are They? that yr arrival
"in Amurka from 1970-2000 threatens our Amurkan
"core of identitas & culture / bc ye don't SPIC ENGLISH
"ye spic to yr enclaves of like-spiccin spics
"quit crying / ye don't wanna assimilate
"ye wanna make babies / ye want me
"to remake my life into some Amurkano Dream—
"¡bullshit! THERE'S ONLY ONE AMURKAN DREAM
"CREATED BY WASPs / BEANERS CAN SHARE
"THAT DREAM ONLY IF THEY LEARN ENGLISH"
. . .

                                  sniff sniff / sniff

"¿nuthin to sey? tha's wha' I thot / thanky for yr time
"& heart yr freedom or get yr ass out"

¿& how 'bout some applause for our special guest class?

Chaley sown pain in O Xochitl's corazón

her pixilated fishnets
& bien crudo yeah please believe
in one heartbreakin mexcoatl   cloud serpent

& upon return to AKlaska / AKlaska Chaley's apt burned to earth / pero y / alas
   & lo / look: burst into bloom
     his body:
        1st blueflint—then whiteflint
              then—yellowflint
      4th time: redflint /
         5th blackflint

that really happened

poor fair Xochitl Flores—Xochitl Xochitl
  yn tetencuacua Xochitl
  temacochihuia Xochitl
Chaley wd be
  her cana al aire—escaping her gringo esposo—
  uncuffing herself from him
  for an aventura w/ an artist—
        ¿quizas? ¿artist? well—
         minor(ity) poet[53]—

verdad—y
Chaley had only
to bend his finger
in even hintest of beckon & words
/ cantos floridos / spilled
sweet scents—
& articulation is more
than a manner of gritting the pendulum

& we musn't forget
¡great jumpin cholla biznagas!
THAT SHE KILLED HIM
sacrificed him to her heathen gods
egad—O guard us sweet baby Chuy—
how he was a genius on that dang redova—qué chingual . . .
how she sent him to McTlán:
how that really happened:

---

[53] "The person who really writes the minority work is a secret writer who accepts the dictates of the masterpiece."
Bolaño

C (c x/c [cc/x]) C/X (¡!)

(when one Xochitl social slept reality)

C one raw youth acquired *ad quaerer* one blue Amurkan grasshopper *Schistocerca Amurkana* jumping / chirping insect allied to the locust / cricket / katydid / *familia Orthopetra* / / for X / warmly/ C / blotto / slightly / kept it / that hopper / inside one halfpint / widemouthed Mason jar / purchased 25-cents sans tax from Salvation Army over on Stedman just below Donnie / the totem carver's apartment / C kotowed X / vehemently / see "The Papilliad" & fragment below / / C posited sd jar on X's mother's / the Beast Master's / PG for sorcery fun / 1982/ MGM / 118 minutes / / front porch / yellow house/ candles / electric/ white / in windowsill / stray cat w/ one blue eye beshrewing C / C exuviated as if C casts off C's teeth / coat on a stick / shell / *sciell* / skin / stick C tapped on X's bedroom window w/ / yesterday / when X wasn't home / C cdn't reach the window so high up [so *heah* up] so C used the stick descried on the road / funambulated C's way along the long thin jutted rock fence gnashing teeth / stretching for the secondfloor window / C wd leave leaves of grass inside sd halfpint widemouthed Mason jar which later burned as the home burned / grass luxated from the lush park overlooking dear Deer Mountain behind X's house / occasionally C wrote poems / pomes [sic] C sold one pennyeach [sic] along the quay nuncupating the moon / groping luna / for / to / as X / X never read / C knitted X one fine #9-stitched sweater / C held the door / meticulous / C divided half of everything C owned / rented a storage locker down by the dock's mouth / C concatenated every artwork / *Gestaltungsarbeit* / viewed / tasted / as recalling X's mother's good eye / her unpatched eye / X's mother / fishpirate's mother or the *Beast Master* / PG for fantasy adventure / bestowed upon C / *gratis* / a scarf for Xmas / read C's X-dedicated epic "The Papilliad" / from the middle out / & silently animadverted C's art:: "Eclectically conservative" / "*glacé*" / "too will-to-possessive" / C higgled "the middle of the night" Tuesday & craved X more than Thursday / afternoon swishing cold coffee cheek to cheek / swiveling in C's solid seat inside the New Yorb Café / before "allegedly" burning down X's mother's / Beast Master's / PG for sword unsheathing / home / ¿to tepefy?/ home is where ye are / X needed / ¿unyielded? / C quavered / after another unfiltered cigarette / C parleyed nominatives/ variables/ *et cetera* / restless C / sky buckled & C

The Pocho Codex

adored / burnished buildings / mountains / fog's light / cloud curtains & wishes to clinch / *vernietung* / X into a neon ball / C wrote on a napkin *inside this life X I moot myself mostly alone X I find myself osculating . . . our axes* / axis—pl / *unawares interloc* / here the text vitrified / C never spoke to X in AK but saw her anyway / / X met C / again after Vegas / briefly & w/o speaking / & on Halloween C told X's mother / upon passing / slightly blotto / she resembled the Beast Master / PG / "The courage / *ferox* / of an eagle / the strength of a panther / & the power of a god" / bc she sported a bow / as in bow & arrow / & C asked where her sack of ferrets lurked / X's mother sd I'm an archer not the Beast Master / as in gee I haven't any ferrets / nor seen that PG flick / X's mother asked C if C knew her child X & C sd "kinda" & that everyday C thought abt how he knew her once in his life but really he only thought that & abt Vegas & visions then & now in AKlaska he cd think of only how he bought coffee from X & always left a tip in X's jar / not widemouthed nor Mason / bc C knew X worked hard for what little X earned / & since she didn't recognize him he felt further compelled to tip her / even though C & X had been formally introduced X's mother found that slightly sweet despite C's lazyy eye & blue Amurkan grasshopper fetish & reputation / as a mediocre poet / she pulled C's arm gingerly & re-introduced C to now uninterested X / now uninterested X to C & C referred to the state of AKlaska as X

that blue Amurkan grasshopper died / alas / hearing the wind of C's breathed breath inside X's head/ X believed X might . . .

X left w/o another word to sey / C's *nom de plume*: C (c x/c) C/X

C sensed

X

down by the green sea / X sat at the edge where C wanted to be

X smelled C on X's hand after once pithily pressing palms

X loved C on the strength of the absurd she read from Søren K

softly C whispered these rash words: . . . *yr ghostly . . . I scrape my tongue . . . brow beating . . . as bubbles travel down yr back . . . l— . . . identification . . . bleaching bleeding of one yet still shadow . . . big enough umbrella for two so why not share & maybe grab some ribs over on 125th at this little . . . one new letter us that's unison baby /*

like two screws holding up the medicine chest . . . birdsong yr face . . . r . . .

at night X saw C's eyes / & saw herself in her mother's patched eye via the unpatched & how

they chortled fire & X reaffirmed X's passion / thus / X still thirsting

state of AKlaska

AKlaska

how sunlight glistened in rainpuddles / walked up steps forcing fresh fishy air into lungs / youth

& beauty

instead X purchased a new Metro card / X traveled the train / X's head mostly down / rain

rained down / wind / not X's breathed breath / αναπνεσμένη αναπνοή / beat down on X's

hood / mostly brown / blown down / flayed umbrella on the sidewalk / skeleton of its structure

unconcealed / X found her own jar / not onepint / widemouthed / nor Mason / nor filled w/ C's

tips / but no new blue Amurkan grasshopper / X picked up a bass at a pawnshop & advertised a

band / X stepped in shit / *scite* / train sd something to X but X understood not what X walked

that straight line

Beast Master / PG for loincloth / corny dialogue[54] / wondered what went wrong / what went

wrong

from "The Papilliad" / salvaged scrap /

> *whispering windless*
> *whistles imagine C eye*
> *(patched) coral snakes*
> *made up fancy dancing*
> *spoons lapping sugar by the*
> *handful O mercy mer-SE*
> *which head leads here*
> *imagine me daily gripping*
> *Agrippa's gathered flushed*
> *rose toilet bowls my country*
>
> *& the intense insurgent*
> *nationals*

by buildings / liquor store compelled X to enter & buy a Coke / it's almost night / X / fuzz

slowed to crawl / X just might . . .

---

[54] **Dar:** I've never seen a . . . pilgrim . . . who wd use a staff the way you did.
Seth: Ah/ but sir/ all pilgrims share a deep love of life—especially their own!

before this C / X had resolve / *resolvere* / & strength / *strengthu* / X alone / solo / this fortified C / C alone sat by the water preparing verses / via typewriter / the moon / la luna / a quarter & supplicating day / C knew X / X entered life before C knew X / yet C knew C wd find X & equate / equivocally/ unknowns/ C truly understood most of all anything / X got that too /

X rummaged thru her fridge / found a beer / early morning / found X's way to C's room / heard the filth / *feculentia* / & fear / ¡O! / in C's voice as C pulled her covers tight

X & the matches . . . & machetes . . .

X woke in a rowboat not rowed & the fogsmoke up X's nose / X sounded a "kh" then a "ks" then rolled back onto X's face facing down / rain globs of marbles beating down / & X's tears

Batos / Bolillos / Pochos / y Pelados

[reconstructed narrative from four notebooks dated April-July 1964 / MS Ketch'kan
Public Library holdings / AKlaska]

no never knew that old man PANCHO Sr who fled
Sinaloa & su vida para viajar his new life solo
for him muy bueno for his wife & chamacos no not so much
but I cannot maynot speak of him as I knew him not
& ergo as man / Mexican / nor pater noster
I have only spicalations abt what & why he did
that big how of how he did
w/ his sallowcheeked absurd & tragic güeroface
his situation equally absurd & tragic

how he invented adventures for himself & made
a new life en Al Norte (always further northward) so as at least to live in some way
this güey / for ye know underground all
direct fruit of consciousness means inertia
or sitting w/ hands folded sitting squeezed
between absurdity & tragedy yet again & do something
or die / dare to narrate & wax poetic . . .

      & ungrateful biped / & ¿what's
better? / do / do nothing / do nothing más
but glitter w/ inactivity / make yr poetry
sparkle w/ anti-depth / live that / & visage
Pancho's visage & his project of refashioning
his image / rebuilding his face / face / helio
rebuilding individual / untruth by reason
of fact /

nay cd never Pancho / play el sancho
dispense his chorizo making children up & down
both sides of that border / all around by Mexkeet bushes
Don Pancho conquered w/ his weasel
Don Ponch thought that all fun . . .
PApas con chorizo

some norther
& fatter / forgetful but faithful
in ways they never imagined
& only but imagined / & that's dead
to imagine that / imagined nation
dead / imagine

but dead in Pocholandia w/
el susto pasado
another Don Fulanito
neo nonamed Mextizo
ill Pocho Pancho
pero:

no tiene la culpa el Posho sino quien lo hizo
compadre

cómo serás cabrón

believe: hay mucha movida en Al Norte

pues y chicanadas en canada

que cosa será la muerte

sí güey me picaba las abejas

pero me comí el panal

adentro los escuadrones   **cabrónes**
machetAZtlános de a motones   **cabrónes**
de frente / caribeneros   **pendejos**
en seguida los lanceros   **pendejos**

tuerto&

cuando Pancho Chastitellez ya vio

que no se le concedía

el no demonstraba miedo

ante mejor sonreía

[surrounded w/ words that rained sounds like fire]

decían los Amurkanos—

qué Messycanos tan crueles

[they left all those craniums / hanging on the trellis]

pues ni modo y Francisco Pancho Chastitellez [el primero]

cuando llegó a su destino

dijo: "vengo en agonía

"pues hoy tengo que ser muerto

"dios así lo dispondría"

y: "válgame dios

"¿qué haré yo?"

y: "aDIOS / todos mis amigos

"me despido con dolor

"ya no vivan tan engreidos

"de este mundo engañador . . .

"aDIOS mi tierra afamada   Sinal♡a

"recintos donde viví

"aDIOS mi querida esposa

"yo me despido de ti"

        ¡ viva Mesico !

        ¡ o pueblos bendios de dios !

llora el mar y sus arenas

lo que yo estoy padeciendo

llora la pluma escribiendo

negras lágrimas de penas

la amo y malhaya mi vida

cuando la imagen que adoro

vio pasarme / triste lloro

sin dares por entendida—

        Pancho Chastitellez—born of white & yellow maize [dicen que]

how he composed that first POCHO CODEX[55]—

one formal narrative—fusing couples' garments—

Pancho awoke to tie his shoelaces
to her own—*¡get back sathan!*

—gritoed—jerked back—sunk—*¿estás loca?*

POCHO CODEX / unoriginal

cara / preface to Amurka already /

---

[55] unoriginal cara: calavera stacked upon dusty calavera

written . . . ¡Amurka! . . . brownish/whitish

smell of lands colonized / wealth

swollen by lands filled w/ unarmed / exploited calaveras—

> ¿de veras?

POCHO CODEX inscribed for POCHOS

pochteca / pochtecatl

for these pochos who don't know know how their lineage passes al sur / whether their abuelos

in Makesicko from whom their pocho fathers who came from there ascended [sic]

whether noble fresas of dirty mojaos / they arrived / here / to AMURKA

& married daughters of beautiful Amurkan people

some dignified capitalists / chosen

& Other pochos married poor Amurkan dirtbags

FLOWER SONG from POCHO CODEX / ms 323232.4

ahua yyao ayya yye—

let us enjoy—

> *a ohuaya*

we aint twice on earth—

let us enjoy

& flowers aint taken from McTlán—only borrowed—

> *in truth*

we must go—

flower my song goodbye—

in truth: ohuaya—

O that pathos of ephemerality

yn Chastitellez axictini

quinmahuiztilia iteohuan—

ica on huel huelitini

oquinxico in iyaohuan

ma nohuian yectenehualo

yn Chastitellez tlapaltic

ylhuiltic ymacehualtic

nohuian mauhcaittalo

huelitini in iteohuan

ca icxitlan quintlalique

yn nepapan yaohuan

yn huel oquicocolique

McTlán

& when he arrived this güerita La Muerte grabbed him by his arm & prophesied some
strange space:

> "for when arrived at pais / nueva Yorb & w/ highest aims
> "in this world / to feel co-ways to alleviate
> "legs of fatigue for eleven days of walking hours

> "I am 174 cm tall . . .

> "si afrecso you w/ massage
> "I will darte so you obtain
> "sentirte papi disfrutalo
> "I am warm woman
> "beautiful yr hearth for firing"

well & good sweet & yammy
& into his palm she pressed this bit
before she patted his cheek repeating
"stonecactus fruit Chaley stonecactus":

tall gamecock who won multiple pits / but w/ this Pocho he met one fierce cockerel who
pecked his comb sure enough

she asked him "¿who ye be?"
& he sd to her "I am Chaley Chastitellez"
adjusting his calzones / shifting weight
from huarache to huarache

beyond them narrow trail w/ barbed wire & nopal thickets there
quiet / serene early morning mountain slope
darkness cool / air fresh after long night rain
& to that broad valley below eight barrios
each w/ its own chapel & saint
so forget yr harina tortillas & beans comparable to plucking a handful of eyelashes &
rubbermeat & get yr ham & whitebread—
hahm 'n' ecks—ole—
for here in Mctlán / a place completely w/o consequence   **en serio**
faraway lands of tlapatl / datura stamonium nanacatl / teonanacatl / godflesh
bitter mushrooms which gave fleshy visions bitter sight / washed down w/ a cold
pulqazo
w/o consequence / Death already / then w/o will Mctlán being
complete w/ all modern lucksuries
including plastics / oils / slaves whipped / jornaleros / Japanese internment camps /
KKKs
       &c
& fine panLatinAmurkan hospitalities
 gold overestimated here claro
yes but Chaley Chastitellez : puro
storyteller & La Muerte / La Pelona
cd do nothing but him embrace

& she to rub her baldhead on his shoulders
& there were great rejoicings
& sports for the next eight days / & visions

& vision

& then they went down to the shit
set shit to sail forth on the godly sea
forth Yucatan forth Isla Blanca forth
San Juan de Ulua

burned some copal

& pinche DiAZtlán sowed his pips
           pues he knows too people
           will say these old stories
           have nothing to do w/ history
           [tell no more—]

[but Tío already married La Marcaida / la güera
[& as he ate more she grew thinner]

& Chaley's dead guilt sent him to this Pelona
to her underworld he descended / cast into water
into cave from crag . . .

put yrself in those chords Chastitellez / into snare
let yrself
not escape / yr faults: deadly—destroying / ¡savage!
mayhap ye've retracted . . . ¿or have ye
swallowed yr stench?—¿yr rottenness?
¿yr blackness? ¿yr faith?
ugly
putrescent
rotten

     forth 500 years conqueror:

"I never go back on my word" Chaley sd
to Xochitl: "¿what ye think I am ¿a Mexican?"

& as fog lifts eight pueblos merge
& city squeezed between mountains & sea—hugging AKlaskan edges of rocky island
coast
smoke from setting to setting / obisidianfavlored smoke . . .
           imagine
           dead imagine

& green raw materials of social readymade here hey hey heya / sez some tourist
brushing Chaley's shoulder shrugging as he passes & some gentleman
from this yellow storefront asks if Chaley's
looking for one maybe two quality Ay-Kay handcrafted

embroidered goods made in southeast HAcia
yes longer he stands here in AKlaska longer &
more eloquent he becomes maybe less brutish
& after all this ¿why? Chaley *¿why do ye want to imagine*
that ye conduct yr own train of thought?

for bueno: te la crees muy muy cabrón
little AKlaska in yr stupid soul
shd shutup & lose yr gall
& open those crusty eyes
 & ¿why? b/c why baby why
he ought not—never—
know / thay he cd never—
& he doesn't love
b/c she's probly
her husband's best woman
ever known that brown one
her husband / entirely slack
& careless / likely to lose
everything down to his testicles
& she took care to wax
before coming to him
in la gran manzana
ni modo y
she más o menos
loves rain & him
wants to be w/ him
how he met her in VegAZtlán
she shuckin pearls
from oysters
he made her laugh
w/ his self-mexrecating jokes
KAY chisme

& if he cd if he cd
take back her past
love her antes than
el gringo pendejo
who colonized her
antes / before if Chaley . . .
pues pues pues pues

'pos: what more to say w/ that hoss
y otras mujeres whose
name rhymes nearly
mostly PUES MOSTLY

perfected products & services
changed & exchanged at everfaster
rates / & the knowledge to design
& create value efficiently
again to market / & mark

& market it effectively
& to be becomingly true . . . PERO:

vision   vision incense / dance / drum / vision
intense vision

a donde vas Tenochititlán
a donde vas
no puedo más
eso si que es
S O C K S
¡all common knowledge comin right on thru!
¡mande capitán!
¡en chingakay see!
common knowledge
diffused . ..
goes into land of dead—yr stench / rottenness reaching
entire world—& at that instant
on his pipi: dead condom filled
w/ black beetles / scratching / crawling
& she / La Muerte remains
panting . . . coveting /
thirsting for that
& hungry
for Chaley
"Mister / ye're a goodboy
"but just of yr own volition
"ye defile yrself—dishonor yrself / dirty yrself
"cast yrself into plumpy excrement—into ¡filth!
"b/c ye have found pleasure in vice
"ergo as penis penance do this:
"pass twice daily twigs
"thru yr earlobes
"once thru yr tongue
"esp. b/c of yr adultery
"b/c ye have hurt
"ye have harmed
"yr neighbor
"w/ yr lousy poetry"
La Muerte's voice voice now sumtotal of contrary chords
—kisslurp / & suck that juice—¡O!—music / music
sueñorita / ¡how he mutilates yr harmonies!

DO YOU READ WHAT I SEE

> hours days four lines going / up staircases

¡lo! but soft what luz
thru younder window breaks—

¡yup! símón—it's the east
& Xochitl is the temple
of the sun—

—reading something that stands
for something that stands
for something that ¡stands!
for something—
            —chained—

so Xochitl—y—eeh—
oh—well—aye—
imagine—dead—imagine—
sound—air—trees—
silent times—an isla de mujeres—

> *me vale madre cabrón—*
> *me vale verga güey*
> *—¿ ?—¡ !d—qué chingada*

call of that blood—poder—
responsibility—inevitable destino
clandestine—

herida abierta—subjectivity—
1st world bleeding into 3rd
—& into McTlán—ol five-plus-four itself—transervsing
opacity—& silence—invented existence
so for gone
                        —gone—
este chingón—gone—

"I'm my langwedge"
Anglish pues—

heart in her can't start throbbing—

—¡light!—sweat—smack—
body junctures—& she caves
they cave—into one another—
her body—hands & feet—
noma nocxi

—in Vegas where even the birds speak ethSpanish—

& when they hacen el amor—
they love undocumentedly—

Meshikan enough—
sí shiekano

license my roaving hands & let 'em go—
before / behind / between / above / below . . .
O my Amurka—my Xochitl—

ga-ga-gachupinche—y los
Xicanos son porque xicanan . . .
& on / & on—

ga—

[4th sun]

[ANCESTRAL FRAGMENT: legit copy / MS 51498q-7 Paper ink draft /
November]

. . . diet consisting of
maize / potatoes & other tubers / cress / sorrel & lupin / pondweed
laver & grass w/ yellow flowers / chewing leaves / fungi / edible grubs /
shells / shrimps / crab & various fish / ocelots' eggs / pigeon / duck &
partridge . . .

. . . local rabbit / venison / & dogmeat . . . bravery

of these Messicans sometimes took that extreme form of fighting
wildcats w/ their bare hands & tearing these fierce felines
to pieces . . .

[COAT-OF-ARMS]

quetzal: first quarter
tree w/ jaguar behind it: second quarter
fringed emblem of sovereignty: third quarter
two plumed serpents w/ fringes in mouths: fourth quarter

[ARTIFACT]

bone earring

[ARTIFACT]

drums made of human skins / bones into flutes / teeth into
necklaces / skulls into vessels for drinking warm pulque / w/ this inscribed round their
rims:
when I die—vieja—take my caca if ye can
& fashion yrself a mug w/ this ditty:
if ye thirst for me—¡drink!
& if it stops at the brink
that will be kisses from yr viejo

ANCESTRAL FRAGMENT: legit copy / MS 51498q-7 Paper ink draft /
November]
                                                                    '
. . . may you die of grief . . .
. . . may you be reduced to living like a wild animal . . .
. . . may you wander like a lost soul . . .
. . . may you have to beg for your living or work as a servant . . .
. . . may you starve / shrivel in the sun / go astray & die
in misery as a penniless miserable
cowardly thieving lousy son of a toothless whoring mother . . .

her visage arrived all at once

taking this supposition she's absolutely chaste on account of her violent refusal
to allow herself to be taken in his arms & bessoed like a queen

& they took great pains to locate Icoquih where some god or other originated—
bleed yr ears / prick yr elbos / codo / give yr thanks a dios

ella—belated /
  smiling—   —westnecklaced
  apologetic   rain

blossoms out of shadowy depths

    ¿which sorceress?

ah sí—this—piercing—
        despues bloodletting
        chingouch:

ACT 1
        one fine day
        one certain (other)
        sorcerer w/ a glyph
        on his left
        palm—another on
        his neck—another on
        his foot's sole
        & also on
        his thumb's ball . . .
        w/ his puppy
        pug Michael following
        behind—

ACT 2
        worshipped according to
        afforded wisdom—¡O!—
        to country's neck
        ¡AK! ho—
            burning orbs
        of heaven drown—
                strangled—
                clouds—

cycle which burns
sea's edge /
& sea itself—
mammar—

ACT 3
        —Chaley began thinking

of writing the past
sun:
    he listened in AKlaska & he saw la luna
        [& the centipedes & the gnats]

[NEXT 19 LINES MISSING]

ACT 4

on jueves he—separation of s . . occurred
on viernes he—made all things
on 1 monkey—working of everything began
on 12 wind—breath born / no death on it / / /
on 2 peak—hell first tasted—done this day
on monday—earth moistened

ACT 5

& then Chaley & La Pelona tasted one another & thusly
she spake "13 heaps—& 7 heaps . . . make 1 heap"

ACT 6

she sd for his speech to emerge / for he
had no speech

ACT 7

together they took
the uptown 6
to Spanglish Harlem
there to the heart
of the sky /
& took each
other by hand—
& they stood
at the center of 116th
& Lex & divided
their lands—
        this—awakening of world—¡open yr
pinche eyes Manhatta!

ACT 8

& Chaley—there / in his vivid divinity—
in his nebulousness /
by himself alone
& everything he invented
he caused to be born—
his word—in his divinity
he moved to Harlem
which was thus
one great event—

[note: it is v. necessary to know the path that's the introduction to the heart]

ACT 9

> to one who has
> no day to one
> who has no light
> to one who has no nobility
> to one who has no poverty
> to one who has no
> gabachitas to one
> who has no moon
> to one—
>   so then dawn
> / & if that
> indeed he—dawned—
> 13,000 steps & seven
> count dawn
>
> he reddened second that day

ACT 10

> & then La Pelona sd
> she was a god / & it
> may be true she was
> not a god /

ACT 11

> fornication on high—fire's set / sunface snatched away—
> tip of her tongue / came—
> —tip of his tongue dripping / perhaps his brains
> [note: tongue—heart symbol]

ACT 12

> envy seated / her
> walk envy—her
> brown envy / her
> ground envy / her
> heart . . . envy—her
> mind envy her
> thought envy—her
> mouth envy   voice
> of hunger in
> her mouth envy

ACT 13

> no sticks / no stones—no good in his heart—truly cold—
>   his tongue: plaster   stone
>
> he doesn't know what
> will end his sins / & he doesn't know he has them
>   —six rows wide / one jump high

—sun lord's fried egg—
    —¡a huevo! —

"Chaley / go bring me three slices of heaven . . . I've desire to eat it"

—& while y're at it—Sun—buy me two packs
of night firefly far northward—its odor
passes far westward—& gimme tongue of jaguar too

her v. white well-rounded knees & hairy legs shook her cloven hooves chattered

some old words found in his grandfather's papers
in those boxes of letters / & his notes to
Pocho Codex & in the various strands of narrative
uncovered in differing locations   Pancho EL PRIMERO
left him several boxes of unopened materials
before he left / most of these letters he had
to collect in Sinaloa / from his half family
yonder / los vaqueros / y Los Chastitellez
sifting thru these he found materials to smatter
minus those materials abducted lost or misplaced
but it was Pancho EL PRIMERO who thought
Chaley enough to include him in his manuscripts
before Chaley was ever a thought / before
ever born / he wrote Chaley / tho Chaley
had never seen his Tío Pancho in all his splendor
sporting his warrior jacket / woven from nettles
of magüey fibers / yes güey / w/ a flint
of feathers / half bloodred rising from his headdress
his underjacket painted w/ human thighs
hands & forearms & his great cape
w/ severed hands & severed heads & lightbleached bones he looked good
in that one black & white foto C found of Pancho
leaning on that lamppost in Tuxson in that year
of his lord Tezcatlipocho

so he told

1
bc they're hunting wets / shit / so he told

Xochitl don't go flouting all yr semana bracelets at once
w/ yr snakeskin boots y todo at pinche Wallmart

or best keep yr SS card handy just in case—socia

so entonces

& so Xochitl laughs

& earlier that day in Vegas

Chaley noticed under his glass tabletop
                sitting alone w/ his icecold domestic draft

                General D Antonio Lopez de Santa Ana

his napkin on his face / his leg well / god knows where that's at

nice domestic draft / cold / & broadcast on television to his left: sports
he never watched / once at a bar in Tuxson he watched
PBS but that only once / w/ ol Agustín Yabronez de Rioseco
in all likelihood off to make his fortune—great bigheaded
fortress of Mexico / el gringo te chingó
cabrona / to Xochitl / te chingó chingó
now on bullriding / & another screen tractors
pulling big loads of junk really fast & flames
erupting from their pipes

& then Chaley w/o interpreter sd I'd have ye know
that ye've come from distant lands at our lord's
bidding / our Presidente Chuy / who's many many
lords & vassals myself included has sent me
to command yr great princessly fortune & give
up yr sacrifices & stay away from lost gringos—
somber distance too please—stop eathing flesh
of yr neighbors & quit it all w/ all that sodomy
& other things ye do behind yr walls—for such's
the living will of our lord President Chuy Xst
& in these firme Untied States of Amurka—
in which we all believe & whom
we worship—great giver of life & death / bear up
bastarda to Freedomlandia

& Xochitl laughed at this

& Chaley then expounded how heard abt some distant

Tío Taco so-called (& also Father Taco[56] / from he who birthed
Chaley w/ his thoughts)
who worked nightshifts at the university hospital north of speedway as a cook
& one day he showed up at work bien crudo
& wooshy woozy / & as he stirred the boiling menudo
in a ten-gallon pot he slipped / smashing his chin
on the cauldron & loosening his glass eye
which / clarín / chinga que damn / fell directly into
the soup

his insurance wdn't cover the costs of a new one / & since then
that Tío Taco has been one-eyed

further enhancing his gnomishness

true story

& Xochitl: ¿cd ye tell
me more abt our Holy Amurka?
& remained silent staring
at her shoes / or floor
w/ eyes closed—

well then I guess now there's nothing
else I can do cept put up my flag—

& then some drunk güey sitting at bar's furthest corner
sd "make peace w/ this pendejo / lady / & fill
"yrself w/ his jobs & honor our Virgen / & make
"sweet sacrifice of yr red/white/blue bleeding
"body—pos yr heart & blood mi morena—"

haughty words indeed

& Xochitl / w/ authoritas
chalchihuites in her ears—
feathered hair—her
only desire to serve
Chaley & his gods
Chaley her tecle
who already promised
to make rounds
w/ her in the Vegas tiangüez
Xochitl sd to that güey back there:
"know yrself puta madre cabrón
"look out for yrself gordo
"pinche rosepetal tamal"
& proceeded to threaten
to lop off his feet

---

[56] Careful: tacos talk to tricksters

Chaley not surprised
had heard of these Mezkins
from Pancho's letters
& library / of Mezkins
in AZtlán—enmity
deeply rooted
in their hearts /
& such this Mezkin
character of that under
cover of peace
they wd only practice greater
treachery—for they
never kept their word—
whatever promised—

[note: & as his translator / ye Malinche—outsider within / insider without]

looking Xocitl in her eyes
in more or less dyadic terms—unspoken
mind—w/ him
& minimal attention to her eyelashes
& how she cd
turn our Aztec empire
upon itself / state of civil
war brought on—no—
instigated by outsiders—
same ol Amurkan
logic / Puerto Rico / Nicaragua / El Salvador / Panama / Chile / Argentina / Cuba / DR
/ Guatemala / El Salvador / Iraq

& Chaley maybe harbored secret
muddleclass [sic] Amurkan dreams
alignin w/ certain
things & comin to know Quetzalcoatl—
performin certain ethnic behaviors—

2

&
she
Xochitl
before outing
Vegas sola
& encountering
Chaley . . .

Xochitl
publishes her blog
tunes off her dig
music
leaves thru

backdoor / of her
cousins' casita /
screen slams /
lights her way
w/ her keychain
light & approaches
barnwise she
thru her silk
Wallmart panties
she
soft touch be
ticklen her fanny
sitting feels
tonguey
how she likey that
she be
him for he knows
she be thought
for ye also
bygmaster have
it she whispers
before entering
important for her
place
& it meant big
deals yes
to her grass she
weeping
oceseven this hill
sky able to feel her
there:
message

some man tall dark
¿Temo?
ghost
of McTlán
return

from
talltime
Orizaba firm

he
stands

&

chingao / ¿who's
this güey?[57]

---

[57] mira: estay entray
el deecho y
el icho—
eye
oon taycho

¿este maestro
sabe tichar?
¿tichar? ¿eres un tichar?

—¡callete musasho!—

adstupet ipse sibi
uultuque
inmotus   eodem
haeret
ut e tenochtitlan
formatum
marmore
signum . . .

3

no   doubt   some
down&out
Meskin
forced   to   seek
better
conditions   in
Hell Norte—
another wronged
by Amurka's
slow   relentless
pressure
of agricultural /

mineral   /
financial
/ & oil corporate
interests
on   this
Messican's
nation's
entire   economic
&
social/historical
evolution / true
soldier
of
the   rekonkuistsa
&   out   of   his
wifebeater dark
her mind her clitoris to clam   **M A M A S I T A**
calming too much quick now / ay
off   **S   O   L   I   D**
so cold check on her hoss
knowing to explore that
in her most prized CHEEK
down she can please any
man or Mezkin hoss deep down inside
her she wanted woods loved
hosses madder her warm moist arous—

Temo & she both galloped thru precise processions
she dreamt of it when her

husband proposed he loved
silk panties b/c she bent on her knees & toucheyed
almost feels like fingers but when he
lifted her head slowly lightly licking
her clit she Xochitl then looked at her
hosbonde's presence now outside barn window
so far away he always coming supersmart
no she didn't
hossin w/ Temo their family Mezkin hoss
her cousins' jointly-owned Vegas stable
out near National Guard armory & Vegas
fairgrounds
& Xochitl again we must tell no one checked
her voicemail & Temo sd seemon

4

but Xochitl
here in this bar made mouth to this compa
sitting back alone crying into his warmin tecate
& Chaley shd sey there's no truth
ye can know everything / Xochitl
ey hey hey hey there: girl using skirt w/ button-down shirt
quickly she scampers by

 how close & hidden Xochitl & Chaley found themselves so close his
breath on her cheek & tho no music they held plenty
including how she held her breath & shivered
& he thought I'm young old Tio Pancho man sure as hell lived
no life like Virginia Woolf but I cd learn to pick
pockets like this for my daily bread my real living
wages carajo b/c I espeak that langwedge
between myself . . . between my ancestors & myself
& not all verbs nor tenses cover that tension
& she looked at him something nice nice woman
here woman this woman Chaley sd hallo hallo
sure strike me as someone beautiful someone
entirely beautiful for me at this moment

struck   spin   swerve   redbricks beneath   gas   blood
    machine

5

& earlier Xochitl's
world vibrated synesthetically

she strolled in sporting her synthetic fibers
heels in purple syllables YEA &
for before she drove this

freeway / her heels off below
her legs/ lefty toeing her

purple spikes righty maintaining
injection of fuel into her
mighty three-punto-five L
four-banger she
passed roadside skyline sculp-
tures of rocks & plastics

she: artist queen of children
her sublime ruffians
she—incinerates mastadons
she—worms & swords her squirms & chortles
she—saves for rainy days
she—jangles whinny trio of tenors
she—whose eyebrows as nests of swallows
she—fabricates w/o scarring sweet 40 winks
she—one sweet forty winker then indeed indeed
she—ruby-throated hummingbird
she—who combs sea snails near Oaxacan seashores
she—whose shoulders drip dry champagne
she—jangles whinnies in her trio of terms
she—gracious beehive mama
she—engages worrying currents
she—victim of some fambly trauma
she—houses & raises wild ferrets
she—eyelines big brownblack eye

she—lightly singing singing signing
she—lyrical outburst twothree time
she—even eats all natural natural
she—left three ones as tip for her barrista
she—never leaves that much ever
she—felt guilty today &
she—didn't know exactly why after all 'twuzn't
she—who went off lookin to study codex thru glass downsouth
she—stayed home worked around her cousins' casita & to go had to go
she—lightly signing signatures & singing b/c
she—hasn't dramatic ins & outs like Chastitellez outbursts
she—ain't chaotic
she—doesn't have snakes for eye
LA PUTA MUERTE—now she had snakeyes for Chastiteyez
she—onyx lampadhphore Phenix amphore
she—knows little bit less than when
she—started but
she—still knows everything
she—pink anguish now sunk ash now conch resonantly foolish to drink trash gold gash of
unicorn lash naked lank thick junglebush wink flash
she—recollected for praxis—yeh pragmatic

6

YUP: she ye know we worship for she Mamas forth
into godliness see her Great
Mama river & earth & sky to plain until foot
in part park & part parking lot
ravishment & phantasy those
lucky onlookers soaked of subsequent
worth makes me think she thinks . . . review
some tangent what we've thought
our manitas on here claims stylistic representation
sometimes
              this our heroine gets caught
out in rain w/o her umbrella & wet
she gets or pulled back into a choke hold

she—looked down at him suddenly unaware of her brown eyes startling under thick black
mextiza brows yea so

she—s not beautiful exactly sd Chaley but such bonedrawn distinction
    well b/c   anyway he sees

7

a hapless fertile plain
& touching hands ¿ye
listen to Nacho Vegas? ¿*too?*
        muy nice

Regreso

& Xochitl's hosbond hobbling from his snakebit stance
wobbly from all that whitemule he ripped off from his neighbor's garage
back round there in their suburban TUXSON four-bedroom w/
two-car garage home situated in some cul-de-sac space
—referred to by X as "the sac"—
somewhere he walks her out in that undeveloped desert landscape back behind
their backyard fence not so far back but far enough away from neighbors
back far enough b/c he of course "gots" it in his mind to teach sunlit Xochitl couple
things or two & as they pass creosote & nopales on some four-wheel
trails / he sez SIT
& he pushes her down upon the hill of fireants & he holds his pistol
above her jabbed into her left cheek
& don't move goddamnit goddamned slut don't move
pinche puta cabrona & w/ his pistol in his left hand
he crouches to remove her underwear w/ his right
stinky dirty whore he sez & they'll eat that taint from ye
don't cross me slutwhore

& ants crawl up her & tears
big as marbles roll down her face & plop
into redsand
shiverin w/ revulsions
loved away & alone & on

so let her fade away & ever keep away away . . .

            . . . tiger & eagle ¡O Chaley!
    Xochitl humiliated by this gabacho w/ large visorbrow—large mouth
& bloody teeth & fingernails / & this plague of fireants

in this time of handsome nights /
                        much madness / much lust / mucho maas / pos

& Chaley in McTlán
so Xochitl sola & tribulations furthered her

but Chastitellez equaled possessing all suns' brigthnesses then all in that one repeated
word

---

    heartbeats her breath
    bosom heave
    red rose rises slowly

    stop for brief libation . . .

    swounds

now that's comodius

O Xo xo xo xo soooooo cheeeeee   & Maylench eeeeeeeee & Loooo yerna
& sweety wet sweaty death

O armies & doors of perceptions high tide in McAZtlán
upnear near WallMart INCorporated township
high tide & wildwest minds weighing worlds
in worlds
ceremonies of days

En la composición de esta primera edición de *The Pocho Codex* se emplearon tipos Bell, Times New Roman y Garamond.

El cuidado de la edición estuvo a cargo del comité editorial de Editorial Paroxismo.

2011

Made in the USA
Coppell, TX
18 November 2022

86641000R00080